Willia

A Collection of Chirurgical

William Beckett

A Collection of Chirurgical Tracts

1st Edition | ISBN: 978-3-75234-961-0

Place of Publication: Frankfurt am Main, Germany

Year of Publication: 2020

Outlook Verlag GmbH, Germany.

A
COLLECTION
O F
Chirurgical Tracts.
By *WILLIAM BECKETT,*

A N

ACCOUNT

OF THE

WRITINGS

OF

WILLIAM BECKETT,

Surgeon, and *F. R. S.*

V I Z,

I N the Year 1709, He Published, I. *Chirurgical Remarks, Occasioned by the Death of a* CH I L D , *whose* CA S E was *printed* in that Year by *Daniel Turner,* Surgeon. To these Remarks Mr *Beckett* subjoined, *An Account of a* Wound *of the* Brain *by* a Bullet; *with Reflections thereon.* And at the End of this TR ACT, Mr *Beckett* gave an *Advertisement* that He had almost ready for the Press, *Annotations and Practical Observations on the Learned and Ingenious Monsieur* GE N D R O N *'s Enquiries into the Nature, Knowledge and Cure of* CA NCERS .

II. *In the Year* 1711, He published NE W DI S COVERIES *relating to the Cure of* CA NCER S . *Wherein the painful Methods of cutting them off, and consuming them by Caustics are rejected, and that of dissolving the Cancerous Substance* is recommended; *with various Instances of his Success in* this Practice *on Persons reputed incurable. Also a Solution of Four curious Problems concerning* CA NCERS , viz. I. Whether the Cancerous Juice *is corrosive or* not. II. *Whether* Cancers *are contagious or not.* III. *Whether if the extirpating*

2

a Cancerous Breast *happens to be successful, it ought to be looked upon as a Consequence of performing the Operation better than our Predecessors.* IV. *Whether a* Salivation *will Cure a* Cancer.

This Treatise came to a Second Edition *the following Year* 1712: *To which, besides some Corrections,* Mr BE C K E T T *added* TW O *other Problems with their Solutions*, viz. V. Whether *Cancers* are curable by *Caustics*. VI. Whether *Cancers* are curable by *Internal Medicines*. In this Piece all that he promised relating to GE N D R O N is inserted. And to the present *Third Edition* He subjoined, by way of *Postscript*, a very valuable *Receipt* for the Cure of *Cancers*, which he informs us was communicated to him by his late eminent Brother Surgeon Mr *Dobyns* of *Snow-Hill*. He had it from Mr *Pain* a Gentleman of *Northamptonshire*, in whose Family it had been, in the highest Esteem, for above 200 Years. Mr *Beckett* likewise adds, that he transcribed it from the Original *Manuscript*.

At the End of the *Second Edition* of his *Treatise* on *Cancers*, Mr *Beckett* gave an *Advertisement* that "He was then preparing for the Press, *Chirurgical Collections*, which would consist of His own *Observation* of *uncommon Cases*, also, the most curious things relating to Surgery, taken from the Performances of the *German Eruditi*, in their *Acta Lipsiæ*, the *Miscellanea Curiosa, Philosophical Transactions. Memoirs for the Curious, Voyages, Travels, Natural Histories of Counties*, and many other things that would afford useful Observations. In this Collection was to be a great number of Figures of Cases, Instruments, Machines, &c. all curiously engraven on Copper Plates. This Undertaking was wholly designed for the Improvement of the Art of Surgery; and the *Introduction* to it was to give an Account of our famous *English* Writers in *Physic* and *Surgery*, for many hundred Years past."

The great and deserved Practice which attended Mr *Beckett*'s *New Method of curing Cancers*, obliged him to postpone the Publication of his *Chirurgical Collections*, as above recited; and which, upon a mature Deliberation, he changed into a much more extensive and useful Design; and, by Mr *Innys* at the West-End of St *Paul*'s, and Mr *Hooke* in *Fleet-street*, Booksellers, He published *Proposals for printing by Subscription in 2 Volumes* 4to, An Account of the Lives, Characters, and Writings, *both Manuscript and Printed*, of the most eminent *British* Authors in *Physic, Surgery, Anatomy, Pharmacy, Botany* and *Chemistry*, from the Conquest to the Year 1721. To which was to be added, A large Collection of Records, principally taken from the *Tower*, containing Grants of particular Favours and Privileges to the most noted *Physicians* and *Surgeons* by the Kings of this Realm for many hundred Years; whereby, besides other curious Affairs not to be met with elsewhere, the Time in which they lived was to be ascertained, as to several of them, has hitherto remained absolutely undetermined. The whole faithfully collected and reduced to the most exact Order of Time.

This Work was proposed at the Price of one Guinea in Sheets.

Between the Years 1717 and 1720, Mr *Beckett* published in the *Philosophical Transactions*, Three Letters concerning the *History of the Antiquity of the Venereal Disease*. I. To Dr *Douglass*. II. To Dr *Wagstaffe*. III. To Dr *Halley*. Proving *That Disease* to have been *known* and *cured* in *England* long before the Discovery of the *West-Indies*.

Of these Pieces Dr *Astruc*, a *French* Physician, full of the Vanity peculiar to his Countrymen, seems doubtful as to their Proof, because he had never seen the Manuscripts, nor rare printed Authorities, cited by Mr *Beckett*; and treating of Dr *Turner*'s *Syphilis*, speaks slightly of that Gentleman, because he is of the same Opinion with Mr *Beckett*.

From the Publication of a small Pamphlet consisting but of 24 Pages, 8vo, Intituled, "A *Letter* from a Gentleman at *Rome*, to his Friend in *London*, giving an Account of some very surprizing *Cures* in the *King's-Evil* by the *Touch*, (of the Chevalier *De St George*) lately effected in the Neighbourhood of that City, 1721. Wherein is contained the compleatest History of this *miraculous Power*, formerly practiced by the *Kings* of *England*, ever yet made public; the *Certainty* of *which* is confirmed by the most eminent Writers of this Nation, both *Catholics* and *Protestants*, as, *Malmsbury, Alured, Brompton, Polydore Virgil, Harpsfield*, &c. and Drs *Tooker, Heylin*, Mr *Collier*, Mr *Echard*, &c. *Translated* out of the *Italian*." And the following Motto prefixed by the Catholic Translator, *viz*.

King Edward the Confessor, *was the first that cured this Distemper, and from him it has descended as an Hereditary Miracle upon All his Successors*. To dispute the *Matter of Fact*, is to go to the *Excess of Scepticism*, to *deny our Senses*, and to be *incredulous* even to *Ridiculousness*. See *Collier*'s Ecclesiast. History Vol. I.

Mr *Beckett* took an immediate Occasion to explode all these Legendary Assertions, and fully proved the Truth of Mr *Collier*'s positive *ipse dixit* to lye on the other side of the Question, in two Letters which he Published, I. To Dr *Steigerthal*, intituled "A Free and Impartial Enquiry into the Antiquity and Efficacy of *Touching* for the *King's-Evil*." II. To Sir *Hans Sloane* in "order to a compleat Confutation of that supposed *supernatural Power* descending from *Edward the Confessor* to the succeeding *Kings* of *England*. Also, A Dissertation concerning the ancient Method made use of, for the curing *Diseases* by *Charms, Amulets*, &c." To which is added, *A Collection of Records*.

When in the Year 1722, it was feared that we should be visited with the *Plague* in *England*, after it had raged so violently at *Marseilles* in *France*; Dr *Mead* published his *Preservative* against *Pestilential Distempers*. And, among several other *New* Pieces written, and *Old* ones revived upon this Occasion, Mr *Beckett* voluntarily lent his helping Hand for the good of his Country, by giving his Judgment, and Publishing (Anonymously) *A Collection of Pieces* Written during the *Plagues*, which happened in the two last Centuries.

Mr B E C K E T T 's *Chirurgical Observations*, made at St *Thomas*'s Hospital *Southwark*; Published last Summer, were prepared for the Press by Himself, and Inscribed to Sir *Hans Sloane* and the *Royal Society*.

T O

Sir HANS SLOANE.

Honoured Sir,

T H E last Paper Mr *Beckett* ever wrote, was an Address to you for a private Favour; in which he says, he likewise had reason to believe that Dr *Mead* would be his Friend. He therein acquainted you that he had, "contracted such a Cold by sitting to write, with his Neck against a North-Window, as he feared would be his Death; and if so, *adds he*, it may be said I dye a Martyr to the *Improvement* of the History of *Physic and Surgery*." Thus concluded his Paper which he did not live to sign; it was found among his *Collections* relating to the *Lives of the British Physicians, Surgeons*, &c. He had copied fair, for the Press, the greatest part of his Papers; and tho' it was an *unfinished Work*, yet from his Character, and the great Pains he had taken, I knew it would be very acceptable to the Public. Accordingly I put it to the Press, and intended to have published it in two Volumes in *Octavo*. Young Dr B * * * *, was recommended to me as a proper Editor: I sent for him and shewed him the Papers; but soon found, that he was much too young both in Character and Ability for such an Undertaking. I printed one Sheet, in *Octavo*, (of which there were but two Copies taken off) upon this, Dr *Milward* informed me, that he had been for some Years compiling *An Universal History of Physic*. He expressed his Desire of purchasing Mr *Beckett*'s Papers, and being fully convinced, from his Learning and Candour, that he would do Justice to the *Author*'s Memory, I readily let him have them. And Sir, that you, might in some measure be apprized of Mr *Beckett*'s PL A N , I have to this Volume prefixed his Introduction to the Work.

I Remain,

Honoured Sir,

Your Most Obliged,

And Obedient,

Humble Servant,

E. CURLL.

INTRODUCTION

TO THE

HISTORY

OF

PHYSIC and SURGERY.

Concerning the Antient State of Learning, and the Antiquity of the Practice of Physic *and* Surgery.

*B*RITAIN has been very happy in furnishing the World, in very early

Times, with a great Number of famous and learned Men. Of the first Sort were the *Druydæ*, who, it is said, had their Original and Name from *Druys Sarronius* the fourth King of the *Celts*, who died *Anno Mundi* 2069. Next the *Bardi*, who celebrated the illustrious Deeds of famous Men, who had their Name from *Bardus Druydus* the fifth King of the *Celts*. *Cæsar* assures us, (and a noble Testimony it is) that the Learning of the *Druydi*, was first invented in *Britain*, and from thence transferred to *France*; and that, in his Time, those of *France* came over hither to be instructed. A celebrated *German* Writer, as quoted by Mr *Ashmole* in the Prolegomena to his *Theat. Chem.* says, that when the World was troubled with Pannonic Invasions, *England* flourished in the Knowledge of all good Arts, and was able to send her learned Men into other Countries to propagate Learning: And instances in *Boniface*, a *Devonshire* Man, and *Willeboard*, a *Northern* Man, which were sent into *Germany* for those Purposes. Mr *John Leland*, a famous Antiquary, in the Reign of King *Henry* VII, who was excellently well acquainted with our *British* Authors, assures us, upon his own Knowledge, that we have had a great Number of excellent Wits and learned Writers, who, besides their great Proficiency in Languages, were well acquainted with the Liberal Sciences. And Bishop *Nicholson*, in his Historical Library says, I think we may without Vanity affirm, that hardly any Kingdom in the World has out-done *England*, either in the Number or Goodness of her Authors; and that even in the darkest Ages our Lamps shone always as bright as any of our Neighbourhood. When School-Divinity was in Fashion, we had our *Doctores Subtiles, Irrefragabiles, &c.* But as the History of the Learning of this Nation in general is not my present Design, I shall confine myself more particularly to what relates to Physic and Surgery. An Historical Account of the Antiquity and Progress of which Faculties, with the successive Improvements they have received, has not hitherto been attempted by any Hand. And indeed the Difficulty which must attend an Undertaking of this Nature, must be very great, by reason of the little Knowledge we are able to get, in this Kind, from those Manuscripts which yet remain among us. The ancient *Britains*, who went without Cloaths, may be very well presumed to live without Physic; but external Accidents they must be liable to, as well in their Wars as from other Causes; and History informs us, they had Methods of Cure for such Misfortunes. The *Saxons*, while they possessed *England*, had their Leeches, a sort of Surgeons, but very little skilled in Methodical Practice. But under the *Normans* that Science began to be much more improved. About this Time the *Monks* and *Fryars*, and others in Religious Orders, out of a pretended Charity to their suffering Fellow-Creatures, intruded themselves into the Practice of Physic and Surgery, and continued it many Years, notwithstanding the Decree of the Council of *Tours* in 1163, where Pope *Alexander* III. presided; which forbids any Religious Persons going out of their Cloisters, to hear the Lectures in Law or Physic; and that it is absolutely forbidden, that any Sub-Deacon, Deacon, or Priest, exercise any Part of Surgery in which actual Cauteries or Incisions are required. Most of the Physicians who practised in *England* about this Time, were likewise well skilled in the Mathematics and other Parts of Philosophy; but the Surgeons of those Times were so much addicted to Astrology, as make some Parts of their Writings very obscure. After this both Physic and Surgery began to flourish much more, by the public Encouragement given very early by many of our Kings to several of the Practitioners in both Faculties, as will appear by the List of our Kings Physicians and Surgeons, to be inserted in it's proper Place. *Hector Boëtius* informs us, that *Josina*, King of *Scotland*, who lived above a hundred Years before our Saviour, well understood the Nature of *Scotch* Plants, and their Use in Physic and Chirurgery; and *John Bale*, afterwards Bishop of *Ossory* in *Ireland*, assures us, he wrote a Book, *de Herbarum Viribus*. *Buchanan* relates, the *Scotch* Nobility were anciently very expert in Chirurgery, and it is particularly remarked of *James* IV, King of *Scotland*, *Quod vulnera scientissime tractaret*. It is said, that when *Scribonius Largus* attended the Emperor *Claudius* in his Expedition to *Britany*, he wrote a *British* Herbal, or Description of divers Plants in this Island. And our most learned and famous King *Alfred*, is said to have written a Book upon Aristotle *de Plantis*. *Cinfrid*, a famous Physician, is mentioned by that early Writer *Venerable Bede*, in his *Histor. Ecclesiasticar.* page 307, 308. And *Ernulphus*, another eminent Physician, in the Time of *Nigellus*, the second Bishop of *Ely*, is likewise recorded in the *Anglia Sacra*, Vol. I. p. 625. Many more Particulars might, in all Probability, have been met with relating to my present Design, had not one very great Misfortune attended the Suppression of the Abbies, which was the Destruction of a prodigious Number of Manuscripts. *John Bale*, before-mentioned, though an utter Enemy to Popery and Monastic Institution, remonstrates against this Piece of Barbarity, in pretty strong Terms, to King *Edward* VI. Covetousness, says he, was at that Time so busy about private Commodity, that public Wealth was not any where regarded. A Number of them, which purchased those superstitious Mansions, reserved of those

Library-Books, some to serve their Jacks, some to scour their Candlestics, and some to rub their Boots, and some they sold to the Grocers and Soap-sellers, and some they sent over Sea to the Book-binders, not in small Numbers, but at Times whole Ships full. Yea, the Universities of this Realm, are not all clear in this detestable Fact: But cursed is the Belly which seeketh to be fed with so ungodly Gains, and so deeply shameth his natural Country. I know, says he, a Merchantman (which shall at this time be nameless) that bought the Contents of two noble Libraries for forty Shillings Price; a Shame it is to be spoken. This Stuff hath he occupied instead of gray Paper, by the Space of more than these ten Years, and yet he has Store enough for these ten Years to come. A prodigious Example is this, and to be abhorred of all Men, which love their Nation as they should do. Yea, what may bring our Nation to more Shame and Rebuke, than to have it noised abroad, that we are Despisers of Learning? I judge this to be true, and utter it with Heaviness, that neither the *Britons*, under the *Romans* and *Saxons*, nor yet the *English* People under the *Danes* and *Normans*, had ever such Damage of their learned Monuments, as we have seen in our Time. Our Posterity may well curse this wicked Fact of our Age, this unseasonable Spoil of *England's* most noble Antiquities. *Bale's* Declaration upon *Leland's* Journal, published 1549. And Dr *Thomas Fuller*, in his Church History, speaking of the same Thing, tells us, Divinity was prophaned, Mathematics suffered for Correspondence with evil Spirits, Physic was maimed, and a Riot committed on the Law itself. However, notwithstanding this Devastation which was then made among our Manuscripts, our Colleges, and some of our Libraries, will furnish us with a great Number relating to almost all Parts of Learning: Some of which, more especially the most ancient ones, I shall here first give a Catalogue of, and then some more modern ones, confining myself to those which more especially relate to Physic and Chirurgery. And, first, we have in the *Norfolk* Library, belonging to the Royal Society,

Libellus de Arte Medicinali in Lingua Pictica conscriptus. And in Cottonian Library,

Præcepta nonnulla Medicinalia; partim & Divina ad dierum rationem Saxonice. Galbe. A. 2. 3. 1.

Exorcismi quidam & Medicinalia; partim Latine partim Saxonice. Galbe. A. 2.

Medicinalia quædam Saxonice & Latine Vitel. B. 3. 4.

Herbarium, Latine & Hibernice ordine Alphabetico. Vitel. F. 14. 34.

Tractatulus de Morbis, Latine & Hibernice mutilis initio & fine.

Astronomica quædam & Medica Literis Saxonicis Membr. in Corpus Christi Coll. in Oxon.

S. Dustan de Lapide Philosophorum. In the same College.

Tractatus Botanicus in Lingua Cambro-Britannica. In Jesus Coll. Oxon.

Medicinales Quæstiones Magistri Henrici de Wynton super Isagogen Joannitii. In New College Library in Oxon.

Liber Phlebotomiæ. By the same Author, in the same Library.

Tractatus de effectibus quatuor Qualitatum, secundum magistrum Ursonem. In New College Library.

Practica Chirurgiæ. Tho. Sculling, continens quatuor partes. In New College Library.

Guilielmi Scoti Medici Watlingtoniensis celeberrimi Liber de differenciis Urinarum.

Joannis Ketham Chirurgia parva.

De Virtutibus Herbarum & notabila Chirurgica.

Liber rerum Medicinalium quondam spectans ad Pharmacopolam Edw. IV. Regis Angliæ in quo continentur Medicamina quam plurima pro Rege & Magnatibus præparata. In Mr *Hen. Worsley*'s Library.

William de Pine, his Chyrurgery.

Receipts and Observations for curing Emrods, Fistula's, Leprosy, Aches in the Joints, Tetters, Worms, Cramps, and *Noli me tangere*, in a very ancient Hand. By *Robert Williams* of *Cockwood*.

A Treatise containing the whole Rules of Physic and Surgery, *M. S. Vetus.* Formerly in Dr *Tyson*'s Library.

Medicines of Master *Willeam du Jordyne*, given to King *Henry*, Regent and Heuter of the Reume of *Fraunce*. In Mr *Thoresby*'s Library.

A approbat Treite for the Pestilence, studied by the grettest Doctours of

Fysick amongs Thuniversitie of Cristen Nations yn the Time of St *Tho.* of *Canterburie.* In the same Library.

A Book of Surgery, wrote in the Year 1392. Divided into three Parts. The first of Anatomy. The second of Wounds, Imposthumes, Dislocations, and Fractures of Bones. The third, the Antidotary of Surgery. Formerly in Dr *Tyson*'s Library.

Friar *Theodore Chalk*'s Chirurgical Receipts, on Vellum. Dedicated to Archbishop *Valentine.*

Here beginnen gud Medicenes for all Yevels yat any man may have yat gud Leches have drawn out of ye Bokes yet Galien Aschipeus Ypocras hadden. For yai were the best Leches yat were in ye World. On Vellum, in my Possession.

I proceed now to give an Account of some of our early Writers, besides those already mentioned. And first of *Maugantius*, who was by Birth a *Briton*, a famous Physician and Mathematician; who, says *Leland*, for his eminent Learning, was made President of a noble College (in those Days) of two hundred Philosophers; which *Geofrey* of *Monmouth* extols to the Skies, under the Name of *Legionum Urbs*; which *Bale* supposes to be *Chester*, excelling all other *British* Cities, at that Time, in Wealth and *Roman* Structures. This Place being most pleasantly situated, Astrologers, and other Artists, settled in it to observe the Motions of the Stars, and undertook to forewarn Mankind from the Comets, and certain Indications of the Planets, what should come to pass. Hence *Maugantius*, said to be superior to all others in this Art, being questioned by King *Vortiger*, whose chief Physician he was, about the prodigious Conception of *Ambrose Merlin*, after a Recital of various Philosophical Reasons, did, at length, it seems, give him Satisfaction therein. This Person, who was the most renowned Scholar of his Country, and who is said to have composed several Books, flourished in the Year of Christ 470, when King *Vortiger* was much distressed by the invading *Anglo-Saxons.* I have before observed, that there were several Dignitaries of the Papal Communion as well as those of inferior Orders, besides the *Monks*, who very early took upon them to practise Physic; and that they were absolutely forbid to exercise that Profession, by the *Roman* Assembly, in 1139. Of this Sort was *Frabricius*, or *Faricius*, as he is sometimes written, who practised Physic not long before this Time. He was the eighteenth Abbot of the Monastery of

Abington in *Berkshire*; to whose Care *Godfrey de Vere* committed himself, to be cured of a grievous Disease he then laboured under; and, as an Acknowledgment for the Care the Abbot had taken of him, he bequeathed to the Abbey before-mentioned, the Church belonging to his Estate, in the Village of *Kensington*, near *London*, with 240 Acres of Land, *&c.* which was confirmed by the King; a Copy of which Grant will be given in the Antiquities of that Town, and the History of it's Abbey. This Abbot departed this Life the VIIth of the Calends of *March, Anno* 1117. Soon after him flourished *Athelardus*, a Monk of *Bath*, who was so diligent in searching out the Mysteries and Causes of Natural Things, that he deserves to be equalled with some of the ancient Philosophers. Having a very promising Genius, while very young, and continuing, as he grew up, to improve his Parts, and fit himself for great Affairs, he left his native Soil, and, with much Alacrity, went to visit foreign Parts. In his Travels through *Egypt* and *Arabia*, having found many Things he sought after, he came Home again with good Fruit of his Labours and Improvement of his Learning. He was, without Dispute, in Philosophy, Astronomy, Physic, Mathematics, and Rhetoric, no ordinary Proficient. Some of his Works he Dedicated to *Richard*, Bishop of *Bayeux*: In the first Work he treats of the Principles, Qualities, and Effects of Natural Things, against the vain Opinions of the old Philosophers. In the Preface it appears, he wrote in the Year 1130, under the Reign of *Henry* I. I might here enlarge upon the great Fame and Merits of *John Giles*, a Native of St *Albans*, who made such Progress in the Study of Physic, that he was made Professor of that Faculty at *Paris* and *Montpelier*, and Physician to *Philip*, King of *France*. After his Return to his own Country, he was, according to *Matthew Paris*, consulted by *Robert Grosthead*, the learned Bishop of *Lincoln*, in his last Illness; of which he died in 1253. He has written, *De re Medica*, and *de Prognosticis*, and some other Things. He flourished about the Year 1230, in the Reign of King *Henry* III. *Hugh de Eversham*, deserves in this Place to be remembred, who was a Man of great Learning, a Physician by Profession, and perhaps the best of his Age. He was well known in many Countries, being a great Frequenter of the Universities. With the severer Studies of his Art, he mingled the pleasant Science of the Mathematics, and particularly Geometry and Astronomy. This made him known to many in *France* and *Italy*, and among the rest, to Pope *Martin* IV, who invited him, by Letters, to come to him, and solve some Questions in Physic, which were then newly started: Accordingly he went without Delay, and performed what was required readily and learnedly. He published *Super Opere Febrium Isaac. Medicinales Canones. Problemata quædam*, and some other Things. He flourished the Year 1281; when he was created Cardinal Presbyter of St *Laurence*, by the said Pope *Martin*, in the Reign of *Edward* I. He is said to have died by Poison at *Rome*, *Anno* 1287; although *Cicæonius*, to palliate this Matter, says he died of the Plague.

Chirurgical Remarks

ON

A WOUND of the HEAD

RECEIVED

By a CHILD from the Blow of a Cat-Stick in throwing at a COCK on
Shrove Tuesday, 1709.

Addressed to
Mr *W I L L I A M C O W P E R*, Surgeon.

S I R ,

I do not question but you have had the Curiosity to read over a very
remarkable Case in Surgery, not only upon Account of the Recommendation
the Name of the Author2_gives it, but partly because I know you have been
for a long time of opinion, That this Age wou'd distinguish it self by the
Advances that *Medicine* has, and will receive; I need not observe, to a Man of
your Capacity, how just, according to my Opinion, our Author has been in
relating all the Particulars of the Case he gives us the History of: Nor need I
intimate to you how peculiarly the Prescriptions were adapted to the several
alterations that were observable in that little Patient: I will only take the
freedom to make some Remarks on a considerable Circumstance, which
perhaps we shall find obstructed so methodical a Procedure, in order for a
Cure.

Our Author is of opinion, *That his Death was owing to the effused Blood from*
some Vessel upon the Pia Mater, *which had been ruptured by the Concussion*
or Shock of the said Vessel, from the Force of the Blow; which Blood pent in
(for want of a Discharge) had formed an Abscess, thereby deluging the
Surface of the Brain with Matter: And this, tho' continually draining off thro'
the Orifice in the upper Membrane, yet some part thereof lying beyond the
Elastic Power of the said Membrane to raise up, and out of the Reach of

Medicine to deterge and mundifie, was at length imbibed by the Vessels, where missing the Salutary Crisis, sometimes observed in the Empieme and Pleuritic Cases, it was conveyed by the Circulation to the Heart, and at length, we are to suppose, somehow effected the Nervous System, bringing on the fatal Spasm.

Thus you see, *Sir*, how plain and consequential the Account of the Child's Death is; but even here, I hope, I shall do no Injustice to the Author, if I inform you, I cannot perswade my self that the Matter was imbibed by the Vessels, purely because *some part thereof lay beyond the Elastic Power of the* Dura Mater *to raise up, and out of the Reach of Medicine to deterge and mundifie*, as our Author's Words are; but that it is reasonable to believe, that some part of it was reassumed by the Vessels, when it could no longer discharge it self as before; for if you will give your self the trouble of looking back to the 32d Page, you will find, that no sooner was the *Orifice choaked up by a caked Matter*, but the mischievous Effects of the Suppression of the Discharge soon began to discover themselves by the Rigours the Child was attended with; and we find our Author soon after fearful of such a thing.

By this we may see how circumspect we ought always to be, lest we interrupt the Design of Nature when she is about to expel any morbifick Matter, the ill Effects that attend it oftentimes discovering themselves after different Manners; We look upon a continued Discharge of Matter to be, as it were, a natural Evacuation, and that it's immediate Stoppage, without other Means, being made use of to divert and evacuate it, to be succeeded by a greater Fulness and Distention of all the Vessels, as is observable upon the Suppression of the *Menses, Hemorrhoides*, or *insensible Transpiration*, there is this Difference to be observed that the ill Accidents that attend the Stoppage of the Discharge of Matter are not so much owing to the Distention and Plenitude of the Vessels, but according to the ill Quality of it, 'tis disposed to render the Patient feverish more or less, which is generally ushered in by Rigours, and sometimes succeeded by Spasmodic Contractions.

For a further Illustration of this, we will take the liberty to relate the Case of a Man of about Forty Years of Age, who was for a considerable time incommoded in his Business, by reason of a violent Contusion he had received on the Upper-part of his Left Arm, a little below the Shoulder: After some time it was succeeded by an Apostemation, upon the opening of which I was informed, a considerable Quantity of Matter discharged, which was not of any ill Colour or Smell, the Matter continuing to make its Exit the same way for several Weeks, at length formed a *Sinus*, which might be easily traced to the Upper and Fore-part of the *Os Humeri*. The external Orifice of this was endeavoured to be dilated, but it not only put the Patient to a great deal of Pain, but pent in the Matter, and caused the contiguous Parts to tumifie very much. About this time the Axillary Glands began to swell and pain him, and by their Pressure on the Limphaticks the whole Arm became Oedematous; soon after some part of the Matter made it's way out under the Arm, upon which it almost ceased to flow from the *Sinus* on the upper-part of it. In short, upon this the Patient found himself very much indisposed, he lost his Appetite, was attended with Shiverings, became feverish, and at length died violently convulsed.

On Dissection we found the Surface of the Lungs to be interspersed with blackish Specks, the left Lobe adhered to the *Pleura*, and the *Pericordium* contained a much greater Quantity of Liquor than usual, though its Colour was natural. The Right Auricle and Ventricle of the Heart were very much distended, and the Diameter of the *Arteria Pulmonaris* considerably enlarged: on the Division of the Integuments of the Abdomen, a very large Quantity of yellowish fœtid Matter discharged it self, which was somewhat viscid; we found that the Intestines floated in this, for the Abdomen was full of it. In the lower-part of the Concave Side of the Liver there was a very large Abscess discovered, which contained a Fluid of the same Colour and Consistence with that which we took notice of before. There was an Orifice in the lower part of the Abscess capable of admitting the End of one's Finger; by which, without doubt, Matter discharged it self into the Abdomen. The Spleen was of a very odd Figure: On it's convex Side there were a Multitude of Streaks, that proceeded from all Parts of it, and centered in one Point, which proceeded only from the Disposition of the Fibres of it's internal Membrane. It was almost full of Blood, which in the middle was corrupted, and stank abominably. After it was cleared from the contiguous Parts to which it adhered, and taken out of the Body, it weighed four Pounds and a half.

There might have been something more observable upon the Dissection of this Body, but the short time that was allotted for it did not give us an Opportunity of making that strict Enquiry as seemed to be necessary. *Blancard.* in his *Anat. Pract. Rationalis, p. 252.* has much such an Observation as this which we have related. See likewise *Schenckius, Lib.* 3.

Obs 26. But I do not doubt, *Sir*, but you have made some curious Remarks on Cases of this Nature, tho' I am pretty positive you will agree with me in this, That the immediate Cause of the Death of the Person we have been speaking of, was the giving a sudden Check to the Discharge of the Matter. It was the Work of Nature in this Case (and what she was endeavouring to perform) to disburden herself of those disproportionate and offensive Particles, which by their Continuance in the Body would but have occasioned an irregular Motion of the Fluids, and consequently a Discomposure of it's whole Frame: For the animal Body being nothing else but a Congeries of Canals, filled with different Liquors, it must necessarily suffer very much, and it's Actions be irregular, if any Heterogeneous Particles become incorporated therewith. We must here allow, that in Discharges of Matter of a long Continuance, sometimes the Diameters of the Fibres and Vessels may be so much enlarged, that the nutritious Juices may be thrown out with the other, and so occasion a general Emaciation: But this may be easily rectified at the Beginning, without Detriment to the Patient, by making use of some spirituous and moderately astringent Remedies, to recover the natural Tone of the too lax Fibres and Vessels, and give the Matter a proper Consistence. It is to be observed in such Cases as these are, that the Part from whence the Matter discharges, if it be the Leg or Thigh, first loses it's former Fulness and Dimensions, tho' soon after there appears an Emaciation of the whole Body. Such an Abscess as we discovered in the Liver of the Person before mentioned, we are inclined to believe might have been found in the Child, had the Abdomen been dissected; for several Authors have assured us, it has frequently been observed to be the Consequent of Fractures of the Skull, tho' I am apt to believe it never happens, but when the Matter has received a Check in it's Discharge.

I shall now take the Liberty to observe, that the imprudent Application of Repellents to some Tumours, and inconsiderate Healing of old Ulcers, with the unhappy Method of Procedure, in order to the Cure of some Diseases, very often discover themselves, by their being succeeded by very ill Effects. *Non tamen in omnibus Huxionibus repellentia adhibere licet,* (says *Sennertus*) *Partibus ignobilibus, præcipue iis, ad quas natura interdum humores protrudere solet, ut sunt Glandulæ post aures, & in collo, sub axillis, in inguinibus adhibenda non sunt, ne humor ex iis repulsus ad partes principes & nobiles feratur.*

The same Author informs us in his *Paralipom. ad lib.* 5. *Pract. Med.* of a Boy, fourteen Years of Age, that died upon the Accession of an Epileptic Fit, which was caused by the striking in of the Scab by the imprudent Use of Liniments. And *Baglivi* allows, that the irregular Cure of the same Disease may be succeeded by a Spitting of Blood, an Apoplexy, Dropsy, lingering Fevers, &c. The Healing of old Ulcers, without having a Respect to those Circumstances that ought to precede such an Undertaking, generally lays the Foundation for a Train of mischievous Accidents; for the Patient soon begins to be sensible of an Unactiveness of the whole Body, is sleepy, has a weak Digestion, Head-ach, and is feverish, which is attended with very profuse Night-Sweats; and these we have several times observed to be the Forerunners of the Patient's Death, though sometimes all these ill Accidents may be prevented by an Imposthumation in some part of the Body or other.

Now to account for such remarkable Alterations, in such Subjects, we are obliged to take notice, that here is the Suppression of the Evacuation of a Humour, that had been constantly discharged for a long time; and this, we have before observed, will cause a greater Fulness and Distention of all the Vessels. Now the Quantity of the Blood being very much encreased by the Addition of this viscid Juice, the Celerity of its Motion must be considerably abated, upon which Account it will enlarge the Diameters of the Vessels, by relaxing their Coats, and pass with so great a Difficulty through the Capillary Vessels, that if it arrive at any Part where the Fibres have lost their due Tensity and Spring, it is disposed to stagnate, and produce an Imposthumation. If this does not happen, as the Motion of the Blood continues to be very languid, the Quantity of Spirits filtrated in the Brain will be less upon two Accounts: *First*, Because as the Blood moves more slowly, all the Parts of the Body through which it circulates, will receive a much less Quantity of it in a given Time, than they must have done, had it moved with a greater Celerity. *Secondly*, The Viscidity of the Blood, together with it's Motion diminished will lessen the Quantity of Spirits, according to the 20th and 22d of Dr *Wainright*'s Propositions of Animal Secretion.

Now this being so, it is no wonder to observe such an Inactivity of the Parts, Sleepiness, weak Digestion, &c. to attend a Person under such Circumstances: For the Quantity of Spirits being so much diminished, the Parts can never be sufficiently influenced by them to perform their respective Functions with that Force as usual. To this we may add, that they are in a great measure deprived of their Power and Spring, and Sensation in general is not near so strong and lively. From hence it is evident, that when Nature has found a Passage whereby she may disburden herself of any excrementitious Humours, we ought for a considerable time to give proper Internals, and make use of some other Method, as by Issues, or such like, whereby we may divert the Course of the Matter, which, if I may so say, has been so long together determined to pass the same way. Beside this Advantage which will accrue by that Method, there may be near the same Quantity of Humours evacuated; and so those unhappy Accidents, will be prevented, and the Ulcer cured.

I am perswaded, that it is not without a great deal of Difficulty that we can sometimes divert the Tendency of Humours to a Part; and I can bring several Instances of Sores that have been healed, where the suppressed Matter has discovered it self, by an Aposthume near the Place where the Sore was, a short time after it had been healed.

Fælix Wurtz, who was a very judicious Surgeon, informs us, That it sometimes happens, that in a little time after a Patient has been cured of a Wound of the Head, he feels violent Pains there, which indicates that Matter is collected in the Part. He adds, That many die of it, by reason the Cause is not understood by some Surgeons. This Remark proves, that the Wounds were not kept open long enough, or else that the Surgeon acted imprudently in not making use of proper Means to divert the Tendency of the Humours to that Part; not but it will abundantly more easily happen to those Parts that are depending, and where the Weight of the viscid Fluid will incline it to settle.

I knew a lusty Fellow, about twenty five Years of Age, that had an Ulcer on the internal Ancle of his left Leg near twelve Years: It had been cured three or four times, but he always found himself very much indisposed after it, till it broke out again, and the Matter had a free Discharge: At length, upon his coming from Sea, it was healed again, upon which he was seized with a violent Pain in his Head, Loss of Appetite, which the next Day was succeeded by a violent Fever and Looseness. His Physician ordered, among other Things, a large Blister-Plaister, to be applyed to the Leg on which the Ulcer had been. The Patient recovered; but what was very observable, was, that the Sore the Blister-Plaister had made terminated in an ugly Ulcer, which would not heal, though various Applications were made use of. If Nature had been in this Case compelled, as it were, and forced to a Compliance in the healing of this Ulcer, it is probable the Matter would have been thrown upon another Part, and so occasioned a Disease there.

By this we may see how cautious we ought to be not to proceed in a Method contrary to the Dictates of Nature; for if we do, we consequently disturb her regular Motions, upon which she oftentimes commences a new Work, which, if it does not tend to the Subversion of the whole Oeconomy, there ensues a Permutation of the Disease, by the Translation of the Matter from one Part to another.

It would be impossible to recount all the obscure Motions Nature makes use of to accomplish such Ends: We will only mention some where the Disease has been perfectly changed from what it was before by such Methods. *Mear* gives us an Instance of a Dropsie of the Breast, which succeeded an ill-cured Hydrocele. *Hildanus* observes, that an inveterate Ulcer of the left Leg being unhappily healed up, the Patient died of a Pleurisy some Months after.

To this I may add an Observation of a Man that had an old Ulcer on each Leg, which being attempted to be cured, as the Matter gradually lessened, he was deprived of his Sight. There was no Alteration to be observed in the Eyes of this Person, but only a Dilatation of the Pupils, as is generally observed in a *Gutta Serena*, which was judged to be his Case. In short, upon the running of the Sores, though he had been perfectly blind, he effectually recovered his Sight again.

I will not tire you, *Sir*, with the Recital of any more Cases of this Nature. What has been hitherto said, I hope is sufficient to incline you to believe, that the immediate Cause of the Death of the Child I spoke of in the former part of the Letter was the Suppression of the Matter, which had continued to discharge in such large Quantities so long together. And that such a sudden Stoppage of a Discharge of Matter may procure a Patient's Death, though the Symptoms that proceed may be different. I have likewise shewn the Difficulty there is in Diverting the Tendency of the Matter to a Part, and mentioned how one Disease is sometimes converted into another: But of what Use these Remarks may be I leave you to judge. To me it seems reasonable enough to suppose, that as a regular Method of Practice is not the Effect of a Man's Sagacity, but the Product of repeated Experiences, every thing that occurs may tend, by a proper Application, to the Illustration of the Art. What else has made some Men so famous for their Prognosticks? Had not our great Master *Hippocrates* a Respect to the Suppression of the Discharge of Matter from Ulcers, when he expressed himself thus, *Ulcus lividum & siccum, aut cum virore pallidum lethale est?* And this we have known to be true in several

Cases.

Well then, does not this sufficiently prove, that where we have Cause to fear a Suppression of the Discharge, we ought to remove any Impediment that may embarass Nature in her Work, and advise a proper Method to promote the precipitating the morbific Matter? For so shall we, by joining our Forces with those of Nature, still keep her in due Course; and that when she is grown languid, and departing from her former Measures.

You must excuse me, if I digress a little to take notice of an Observation that some Authors have made, *viz.* That from a dangerous Fracture of the Skull, after Death the Liver has been often found impostumated. They have been likewise very sollicitous to know which way the Matter could be conveyed to so remote a *Viscus*; but it would be needless for me to offer what has been said in this Case, because it seems to be evident enough, that a Part of it is reassumed by the Vessels; which, with that should have been discharged from the Mass of Blood, is by the Circulation deposited in that Part. But here we may start a considerable Problem, which is, How comes it to pass that the Morbific Matter if it's Discharge is suppressed, is thrown upon the Liver rather than any other Part? In order to the Solution of this, we ought to consider, That the Spleen is subservient to the Liver in performing its Office, by giving the Blood a Check in it's Progress, whereby it's Velocity is lessened; otherwise so thick a Juice as the Bile could not be separated from it. Now the Motion of the Blood being rendered abundantly slower in this Part, it is no wonder that the Morbific Particles separate themselves from it, while the Filtration is carrying on, and by their Assemblage form an Abscess in the Part.

You may perhaps expect, *Sir*, that I should make an Apology to excuse the Length of my Letter; but I assure you, the Pleasure I have taken in writing it would oblige me to make it of a larger Extent, if I did not find I should be forced to take notice of some things, which may perhaps have a Place elsewhere. I have only this to add, that if through the little time I have taken to write it in, I have in any part omitted to pay that Respect as is due to you, I shall very readily ask your Pardon. In the mean time I must own my self to be,

Your very much obliged Servant,

W^m. Beckett.

Southwark,
Aug. 22, 1709.

OF A

Wound of the Brain

By a *BULLET*.

To the SAME.

IF you remember, *Sir*, in the History of the *Child's Case*, which I have before mentioned, it was observed, that notwithstanding the violent Pressure upon the Brain, by the depressed Pieces of the fractured Skull; yet the little Patient laboured under no worse Symptom, than a Head-ach, and was in a Condition to walk about the Chamber. This was really very remarkable; but if you will be pleased to give your self the Trouble of reading the following Account, I do not question but you will meet with something much more surprizing.

On *November* the 4th, 1707, it happened, that during an Engagement between a small *English* Vessel and a *French* Privateer, near *Margate*, one of our Men was unfortunately wounded by a *Bullet*, which past through the middle of the *Os Frontis*. The Surgeon aboard the Ship immediately enlarged the Wound, by making an Incision through the Integuments, but could not discover the Bullet; whereupon he dressed him up, and the same Day being set ashore, he was dispatched for *London*. On *Thursday* the 6th Day of the same Month, he arrived, having walked much the greater part of the way in that time, which is about 66 Miles; the same Day his Surgeon endeavoured to extract some Pieces of the Bone, which discovered themselves through that Aperture which was made by the Bullet, but without Success; for they consisted chiefly of the internal Table, which were much larger than the Hole in the external: Upon this the Wound was immediately drest up, and a second Attempt was made a Day or two after; but it proved as successless as the former. In the mean time, the Patient continued to be very hearty and well, and seemed to be no more indisposed than if he had only received a slight Wound of the Head. The opening the Skull with the Trepan was proposed, and which would probably have been put in Practice in a Day or two's time: But on the Sabbath-Day Morning following, after he had rested well all Night, he was seized with such violent convulsive Motions as were very surprizing; during which he expired. The Body being laid on a Table to be dissected, all it's Parts appeared so prodigiously inflated, that the Person, when a live, being one of the largest Stature, it seemed perfectly monstrous. A Puncture being made in any Part through the Integuments, there was nothing discharged but a subtile Matter or Air; immediately after which the Part subsided, though before on a Compressure of the Fingers it would receive such an Impression as is observed in Oedematous Tumours; but it would suddenly return to it's former State. The Surface of several of the Parts appeared livid and vesicated. The Skull being opened, the Bullet dropped out of the Brain, all the Fore-part of which was corrupted, and abounded with a thick yellowish Juice, of a very offensive Smell; there were two or three very large Pieces of the inner Table of the Skull, with some smaller that were found among the lacerated Membranes, and lodged in the corrupted Brain.

This Case is so particular, that it may not be amiss if we make some Reflections on it.

We are very well assured, *Sir*, that it has been a Matter of very great Surprize to several ingenious Men, to consider how the various Operations of the Body have continued to be performed, when those Parts which were so absolutely necessary to the Well-being of the Animal, have been naturally or accidentally disordered to such a degree, as to suffer a perfect Confusion of their Parts: And of this we find Variety of Instances in those Authors, who have very obligingly applied themselves to relate the Histories of deceased morbid Bodies. But that the Brain it self, which is the very Source and Principle of all Animal Functions, should, after it has undergone such a Violation as we have observed, continue several Days without incommoding the Person in the least respect, is really very remarkable; for if we do but consider what an absolute Necessity there is for a constant Supply of Animal Spirits, to empower the

Parts to perform their mechanical Actions, and at the same time reflect on the Disorder and Corruption of that Part, whose Office it was to secrete a sufficient Quantity of those Spirits, we might very reasonably expect a considerable Alteration in the whole Body. One might very well think, that from the Deficiency of Spirits that would ensue, the Parts could no longer continue to perform their Actions, but must gradually lose their Power and Spring, and at length become in a manner destitute of Motion: For we can scarce perswade our selves, that Nature in this Case is so provident as to suffer the *Cerebellum* and *Medulla Spinalis* to filtrate the Spirits in a greater Quantity, that they might supply the Exigencies of the Body.

There still remains some considerable *Phænomena* to be accounted for, as the convulsive Motions, the prodigious Inflation of the Body, &c. As to the former, it may be perhaps accountable from the violent Conflict we may imagine to have happened on the mutual Engagement of the Juice that was found so plentiful in the corrupted Brain, and that which had undergone no Alteration from it's original Purity. Add to this, that the Animal Spirits in the Nerves receiving some ill Impressions by the Accession of some of those impure Particles, could no longer sally out upon the Command of the Will to any particular Part, but must consequently so irritate the Nerves, as to cause their Extremities to contract themselves; upon which Account the Blood becomes imprisoned in the muscular Fibres, which abridging their Length by enlarging their Diameters, the Parts must necessarily suffer involuntary Contractions: At the same time those minute Capillary Extremities, which terminated in the Miliary Glands, were probably so contracted, or crispt up, as perfectly to close the Orifices of the excretory Ducts of those Glands, which are the only sudatory Pores: By this means all that vast Quantity of Matter which is usually discharged by insensible Transpiration, became imprisoned underneath the Integuments of the Body, and so distended all its Parts to such a prodigious Degree, as was observed. This Constipation of the excretory Ducts, and crisping up of the Extremities of the Nerves, might likewise have a considerable Effect on the small Branches of the Arteries and Veins which accompanied them; for by this means the Blood they contained might be obliged to stagnate in the Glands, which must occasion an Enlargement of the Diameters of those minute Vessels; and so the livid Colour which was extended on several Parts might be probably procured: Besides this, the Blood being in such a comprest State, some of its more fluid Parts might be exprest from it, which lodging underneath the *Cuticula*, might make the Parts appear to be vesicated; there is nothing more certain, than that Animal Bodies perspire after Death; or that the perspirable Matter continues to pass off as long as the Body retains any Warmth. This is confirmed by an Experiment of Sir *Thomas Browne*, in his *Pseudodoxica Epidemica*, where he tells us, That "upon exactly weighing and strangling a Chicken in the Scales, upon an immediate Ponderation he could discover no sensible Difference in Weight; but suffering it to lie 8 or 10 Hours, till it grew perfectly cold, it weighed most sensibly lighter. The like, says our Author, we attempted and verified in Mice, and performed their Trials in Scales that would turn upon the 8th or 10th part of a Grain."

I am, Sir,

Yours, &c.

W. B.

NEW

DISCOVERIES

CONCERNING

CANCERS.

ADDRESSED TO

Charles Bernard, Esq;

Serjeant-Surgeon,

AND

Surgeon in Ordinary, to Her Majesty Queen

ANNE.

SIR,

I LOOK upon it as a peculiar Happiness, to live in an Age when Men of our Profession consider, that as the Art is capable of receiving daily Improvements; useful Discoveries, confirmed by Experiments, ought to receive the joint Concurrence of their good Wishes; notwithstanding, they may contradict an Opinion that has been almost universally received. These we shall always find, are the Gentlemen who in opposition to those Bigots whose Tempers discover them to be the Votaries of a few opinionative Men, endeavour to guide their Judgments by Reason, backed with judicious Observations, and whatever Arguments are produced, will never go about to controul Matters of Fact. It is a grand Truth that Necessity gave Being to *Physick* and *Surgery*, and Experience is the only Way to bring them to

Perfection; but it is much to be lamented by them that are Well-Wishers to those Arts that the Persons which are perhaps capable of advancing them most, devote themselves so much to speculative Fictions (the Effects of teeming Brains) that some have pretended with a magisterial Air to dictate, even to Experience itself. In such a Case it would be needless to go about to offer Arguments sufficient to disengage their Inclinations, Time only must discover to them their Error, when it makes them sensible they have, to no Purpose, persisted in the Pursuit of frivolous Niceties; for in reality, the Benefit of Mankind in general is deduced from Practical Truths. The Thoughts of this are sufficient to inspire every generous Soul with an ardent Desire of discovering something that may be of so universal an Advantage: As for my own Part, I was not animated to concern my self in the Undertaking I have engaged in, by a Prospect of gaining that Honour that is often liberally bestowed on those that mint new *Hypotheses*, or make new Discoveries; my only Design was to inform my self, whether some of those Diseases, which are generally reputed incureable, are not actually in themselves curable, and by this means to wipe off a Reproach which has been cast on Nature, when in reality it proceeds only from our own Weakness, and the Infirmity of our Art. A diligent Application to those Distempers which baffle us most, has been frequently recommended by very reputable Authors, and some of those who have obliged us with the Histories of *Diseased Persons*, have very often mentioned considerable Cures, which have been happily performed after the Patients have been looked upon by some as incurable. *Hippocrates* tells us, *Lib.* 2 *Aph.* 52. *Si Medico secundum rectam Rationem Facienti, Curatio non statim succedat, non est tamen mutanda Methodus, quamdiu id restat quod à Principio visum est.* I am fully persuaded that most Practitioners in *Surgery* have at some Time or other, by an industrious Application, been successfull where Art could not warrant a Cure. As to the *Disease* I propose to make the chief Subject of this Letter, tho' it be generally branded with the Character of Incurable, I must freely own I never could discover any thing essential to it in general that should make it so; it is true, there are many *Diseases* that are not to be cured, where certain Circumstances are conjoined, which very much contribute to the Misfortune; tho' Others of the same *Class* exempt from those Adherents may, perhaps, be happily enough cured; Thus for Instance. In *Cancers* we have but little Reason to expect a Cure in a Person that is old, if the *Cancer* has been of many Years standing, and is firmly fixed to the Ribs; but if the Patient be not so far advanced in Years as to be uncapable of receiving the Benefit of Nature by the regular Discharge of the *Menses* and the *Cancer* be loose; notwithstanding, it be Ulcerated, over-spread with fungous Flesh, discharge a filthy Matter, and smell very offensively; we do upon Experience affirm that such a Patient may be cured. We must own we cannot be of the Opinion of the *Paracelsians*, who affirm there is no *Disease* but what is curable in any Patient, for the Reason we have given; nor can we with the *Galenists*, agree that the *Gout*, *Dead-palsie*, *Stone*, *Cancer*, &c. are *Diseases* absolutely incurable; because Experience discovers the contrary. We find that Mr *Boyle* is of the same Opinion, and thinks it were no ill Piece of Service to Mankind, if a severe Collection were made of the Cures of such Persons as have been judged irrecoverable by the *Doctors*; that Men might no longer excuse their own Ignorance by the Impotency of Nature, and bare the World in Hand, as if the Art of *Physick* and their Skill, were of the same Extent. There seems to be one very effectual Way to rescue the medicinal Art from the Aspersions of some bold Persons; and that is that of a certain Number of regular Practitioners in *Physick* and *Surgery*, each of them should apply himself to the Study of one particular *Disease*: By this means we should soon find they would be capable of surmounting those Difficulties that have all along baffled the most Judicious of the general Practicers. How odd, and disagreeable this Opinion may seem to some Men I know not; but I assure you, *Sir*, I find it of a very ancient Date; for *Herodotus*, a *Greek Historian* informs us, that before his Time, the *Physicians* in *Egypt* used to apply themselves to the Study and Advancement of one *Disease* in particular. *Baricellus*, and *Lionardo di Capoa*, observe the same likewise, in Relation to the Practice of *Physick* in that Country. *Baglivi*, in the Scheme he lays down for erecting of Colleges for the Improvement of *Physick*, tells us, that every Fellow of his Literate Society must have one *Disease* allotted him for the Task of his whole Life; and which elsewhere he says is not sufficient for the illustrating the Province of one *Disease*; but that we lie under a Necessity of taking in Materials from all Hands. But there is no Man that we know of, has spoke more agreeably of this Matter than Dr *Harris*, in his *Pharmacologia Anti-Empirica*, he owns that he took more than ordinary Pains in one particular *Disease*, and assures us he verily believes if learned Men, after a compleat Acquisition of the universal Method of *Physick*, and a necessary Search into the Nature and Cures of those manifold Infirmities and Diseases, which, with a kind of infinite Variety, do afflict Mankind, would, with their utmost Vigour and Resolution, prosecute

28

the Knowledge of some one *Disease* eminently above others; they would, most certainly, find a particular Providence attending and assisting them in so good and honest a Design. He adds, a few Pages farther, that wherever a Man's Thoughts are intent and fixed, wherever his Genius does naturally incline, and all his Aims and Application do continually tend, whether it be to pertinent or insignificant Matters; whether it be to useful, or else meerly curious Things; if he has but tolerable Parts, and Education corresponding, he can hardly ever miss; it is hardly possible he should miss the becoming Eminent, and in great Measure perfect, (I mean perfect (says he) according to the Modulum of Human Capacity) in that one Point. But there is one Thing to be recommended to the Consideration of the Person, who takes upon him the Enquiry into the Nature of one particular *Disease*, which perhaps he might be very liable to err in, if not cautioned against; and that is, that he be not too bold and rash in his Attempts; for, as *Galen* says, *The* Physician's *Art is not like that of an* Artificer, *who may make what Experiments he pleases, to satisfy his Curiosity; because if he spoils the Materials he works on, no Body is endangered by the Miscarriage: In Corpore autem humane* (adds he) *ea tentare quæ non sunt Experientium comprobata Periculo non vacat, cum temerariæ Experientiæ Finis sit totius Animantis internecio.* I believe we shall find that one of the grand Reasons, why Persons, generally speaking, have been so negligent in making any Attempts on *Cancers*, has been the seeming Discouragement they have all along met with from Authors. The Caution *Hypocrates* has given us in his Thirty eighth *Aphor. Sect.* 6. has scarce been omitted by any one considerable Person that has wrote of this Subject, tho' perhaps the Sentence has often had an Exposition put upon it, contrary to the Author's Meaning; but of this, more in it's proper Place. I proceed now to give an Idea of *Cancers* in the Breast from an external Cause; and this I shall do without concerning my self with the Opinion of the Ancients; for since we have been so happy as to live in an Age which will be remarkable for the many surprising Discoveries which have been made in *Anatomy*: We should be reckoned unworthy the Advantages we enjoy, if we did not study to apply them to the Benefit of Mankind in general. The more inquisitive and learned Part of the World, are at this time very well assured that the Animal Body is an exquisitely framed Machine, and that it's Composure is little else than a Compages of branching and winding Canals, which are kept to a moderate Degree of Extention, by Fluids of different Natures; and that the Motions of these were first determined by the divine Architect: Thus in a natural State, the whole *Fabrick* is governed by certain Laws impressed on the Fluids; and we often find the unhappy Consequences of the Discomposure of a Part, to discover themselves first by an Interruption of the Motion of the animal Juices. Thus in a *Cancer* of the Breast which proceeds from a Blow or Bruise (as upon strict Enquiry we have found they most commonly do) is it not probable that by such means a Confusion of the true Order of the little Glandulous Grains and their excretory Ducts may happen? and at the same time an extravasated *Lympha* may lodge in such a spungy Texture, which in time becoming viscid, will coalesce with the Glandular Substance, and form a *Mass* considerably compact? Now this being so, it is reasonable to believe that as the Lymphatic Juice continues its Motion till it arrives at the indurated Part, its Passage must be embarrassed there; upon which, it will soon be qualified for an Union with the remaining Part of the glandulous Substance of the Breast; and so the whole be perfectly changed from what it was before. This *Hypothesis* is in a great Measure grounded on Experiments; for if we express a Juice from some of the *Cancerous Mass*, and hold some of it in a Spoon over a Fire, there immediately flys off a small Vapour, and the Remainder hardens not unlike the white of an Egg boiled; this shows it to have the Properties of the *Lympha*; for the Chymical *Analysis* of that Liquor assures us it is a Composition of a great deal of fixt *Sulphur*, a little *Volatile*, some *Phlegm*, and much *Volatile Alkalie*; to which some add a little Earth: Now while the *Volatile Alkalie* keeps the Sulphur dissolved, the *Lympha* remains in a State of Fluidity; but when, by making the same Experiment, the *Volatile Alkalie* is evaporated, the Remainder hardens, and forms a pretty compact, whitish Substance. From hence the judicious *S U R G E O N* may easily deduce the Reason why these Sort of Tumours can never be brought to Suppuration. We shall not be so particular as to mention those *Cancers* which proceed from internal Causes, nor several other things which relate to the former; for what we have here said, we look upon to be commonly the Method of the Formation of them; and as such, we did endeavour to calculate Remedies that should peculiarly operate on the *Mass*, so as to dis-unite the firm Cohæsion of its Parts, and dispose them to separate and come away, without any great Inconvenience to the Patient; which is what we would *recommend* with all the Earnestness imaginable to those that are desirous of discovering a Method of curing *Cancers*. We were before sensible that it was possible for one Body to operate on another determinate Body, without being able to have any such Effect on innumerable Others; as *Quicksilver* will desolve Gold, *Aqua-fortis* Iron, *Vinegar* the Shell of an Egg, *Oyl* common Sulphur, *&c.* which will not have any such Effect on several other Bodies; for there is nothing more certain than that the Operations of Dissolvents are so determined by the various Texture of the Bodies on which they are employed, that a Liquor that is capable to corrode a more hard and solid Body, may be unable to disunite the Parts of one more soft and thin, if of a Texture indisposed to admit the small Parts of the *Menstruum.* It may be expected I should say something in relation to that which is generally looked upon to be the grand Cause of the Incurableness of *Cancers,* I mean the acid Humour in the Blood. But if those Gentlemen who are fond of entertaining this Opinion, do but consider that *Cancers* are often formed in a perfect State of Health; and that during the Time the Cancerous Substance dissolves, and comes away according to our Method, the Sides will run a digested Matter, and heal by the Application of dry Lint only; they will be of my Opinion, that neither the *Atrabile* of the Ancients, the corrosive *Alkalious* Salt of the *Chymists,* nor the predominant *Acid* of the Rest of the Moderns, are capable of procuring those Alterations that *Cancers* are sometimes attended with. If we trace the Writings of our Predecessors to their earliest Date, we shall find that many of them have made Mention of the Roots of the *Cancer,* which they took to be the large blew Veins that are often extended on its Surface; and the entire Removal of these they thought to be absolutely necessary, or the Patient could not be cured: But I believe there is no Body at this Time that considers the *Mechanism* of the Parts in such a Condition, but will agree they are the necessary Consequents of it, and that their Absence, or Presence is of no Importance; that the *Cancer* is sometimes attended with Adherents, or Appendices, which may very well resemble Roots, we are assured; but these generally lay deep, and not easily discovered; the most considerable One that ever we saw was very near Five Inches long, and of an unequal Bigness, some Part of it did not exceed the Largeness of a *Goose*'s Quill, but some others were near as big as the Top of the Thumb, which resembled so many Knots in it, it divided in the Middle, and continued separated about an Inch and a Half, and then re-united, it was of a more tender Substance than the Body of the *Cancerous Mass,* but of the same Colour, and was probably the Juice that was last applied to the *Cancer,* which assumed a Form agreeable to the Cavities it lodged it self in. Such Adherents as these are, I am more inclined to believe, are the Cause of the unsuccessful Attempts on *Cancers,* than any *Acid* in the Blood; for I am of opinion there are few Persons unacquainted with

Medicines that are capable of correcting its *Acidity* when it happens; and had the Cure of *Cancers* depended on that, I am positive they would not at this Time have had such ill Character. We have before shewed that *Cancers* have generally their Rise from a Blow or Bruise, and that when the Body is in an healthful Condition, and the Blood and *Lympha* temperate and sweet: Now if there always is an *Acidity* of the Blood when Persons are afflicted with *Cancers*, the *Cancers* must sometimes cause it, and not the *Acid* in the Blood the *Cancers*, as is the Opinion of most of the Moderns. What has been hitherto said, is sufficient to prove that if Men will be always so sluggish as to acquiesce in the Dictates and Dogmatical Positions of their Predecessors, and not exert their Faculties in endeavouring to undeceive themselves; we must no longer expect our Art will receive any Advancements, but as Slaves to their Opinions content our selves with what we know already. Were not *Parisani*, *Riolan* the Son, and *Plempius*, so much in the Interest of the Ancients, that when our Country-man, the assiduous *Harvey*, had discovered the Circulation of the Blood, they not only opposed his plain Demonstrations, but engaged in vigorous Disputes against him, tho' at the last they were obliged shamefully to recant their Follies. *Celsus* tells us, *Vix ulla perpetua Præcepta Ars Medicinalis recipit*; scarce any of the Precepts of the Medicinal Art are perpetual. And shall we engage then in the List with a few opinionative Men, that ground their Course of Practice on those Methods only, in which they have been brought up, and implicitly assent to the Conjectures of others. No certainly, this would be to strangle Truth, and extinguish the Vigour of our Wits with precarious Authorities. Consonant to this, Dr *Paxton*, in his lately published Treatise, tells us, *Thus Men, out of a trifling Distrust of their own Parts, will not use them; or out of Laziness of Temper, will not employ them, chusing rather to be wise or learned, by being adorned with Others Whimsies, than undergo any Labour, Fatigue, or Trouble of being really so.* I believe there are some Men that would rather contradict their Senses than deny the Authority of a darling Opinion: Of this, we have a sufficient Proof in an Instance, related by an *Italian* Author before-mentioned. He tells us, *That a certain Publick Reader long Time versed and grown Old in the Books of* Aristotle *being one Day present at a Dissection, and clearly seeing that the* Vena Cava *takes its Rise from the Liver, confessed with Astonishment what his Senses discovered to him, but that he ought not therefore, by crediting his Senses, to contradict his Master, who constantly affirms all the Veins in Man's Body to have their Original from the Heart; because, said he, it is much more easy for our Senses to be sometimes deceived, than the Great and Sovereign* Aristotle. I here seriously confess, I have as much Veneration for Antiquity as any Person whatsoever; but it would be ridiculous, if, as One says, we should so far forego our own Judgments as always to follow the Foot-steps of Others, and to be certain of nothing our selves: For this would be to see with others Eyes, to hear with others Ears, and to understand with other Men's Intellects; so that whenever we make Quotations from the Ancients to strengthen our Opinions, we ought to do it judiciously, and fully consider, whether their Notions of Things are consonant to the Experience of these Times. To prove to you, *Sir*, that I have not proceeded to apply my self to the Cure of so formidable a Disease, without a Precedent, I shall instance to you that *Fuschius*, a learned *Italian Surgeon*, had such a wonderful Reputation for it formerly, that some Authors say he was distinguished by a particular Title, which discovered his Success. His Method I have made use of, and tho' by passing thro' several Hands (the Author being mentioned by few) it has been stampt with wonderful Encomiums, I have not hitherto found it deserves it, notwithstanding I did not omit the most minute Circumstance in preparing the Medicine, or prosecuting the Directions; but in its proper Place, I shall take particular Notice of this, and several other Remedies, that have been recommended by some Authors, as substantial and extremely useful; for if in One or Two Instances they have been crowned with Success, by Degrees they are handed down as infallible in all Diseases of the like Form. To the former Account I may add, that Monsieur *Alliot, Physician* to the Duke of *Lorrain*, has applied himself to the Cure of this Disease very successfully, as a *Schedule* he published at *Paris* some Years ago informs us; we are likewise assured by Mr *Boyle* that Dr *Haberfield*, one of the Principal *Physicians* of *Bohemia*, has had extraordinary Success in the Cure of *Cancers*; and the Sieur *Gendron*, Doctor of *Physick* in the University of *Montpelier*, has done extreamly well on that Head; the latter of these Gentlemen I cannot mention, without making an Apology for not Publishing our Annotations on his Enquiries relating to *Cancers* which was promised at the latter End of our Chirurgical Remarks, Printed above a Year ago; but I assure you, *Sir*, I was more inclined for some Reasons to offer what is therein contained, with several Observations made with the greatest Exactness, and to which, perhaps I may have an Opportunity of making several Additions, in a particular Treatise, so that the whole may conspire to finish a compleat Account of this Disease. I had at first a Design of enlarging considerably on this Subject in this Letter by adding various Things, but considering they might better find a Place in what I just now mentioned, and that you did not desire an exact History of the Disease, I resolved to omit them. I shall now proceed to give you some Instances of the Success of our Method, as being what you are most solicitous of, the Cases I shall relate shall be each of them different from the other, for I know you do not approve of that pompous Method of some Persons, that enumerate abundance of Instances of Cures when perhaps there is no great Difference in the Cases or the Method of treating them.

The most considerable Case that offered it self during our first Enquiries into the Nature of *Cancers*, was that of a Woman, who about Four Years before received a Blow on one of her Breasts, upon which it began to swell, grow painful, and after some time became all over livid, and of so prodigious a Bigness and Weight, that she was obliged to keep it suspended by a Napkin round her Neck: But in regard our Method was not put in Practice till by other Applications it was become ulcerated, we shall speak of it as such. The Patient, then, at this time complained of a very violent Pain, which extended it self to the Back and Shoulder, by the Communication of the Nerves (for those of the Breast come from the fifth Pair of the Spine, and from a *Plexus* about the *Clavicels.*) To remedy this, she had taken no small Quantity of *Hypnotic* Medicines, which, without Doubt, destroy the due Texture of the Blood, and so become prejudicial to the Patient, and disadvantagious to the *Surgeon* that proposes a Cure. But because Persons generally find some Relief by Opiates, as they retard the determined Motion of the Blood, straiten the Nerves, and check the tumultuous and disorderly Influx of the Spirits; so, probably, in these Cases, their Use will be continued. Besides the acute Pain, the *Cancer* was over-spread with fungous Flesh, its lower Part extreamly hard, knotty, blackish, and its Basis seemed inclinable to fix; the Matter which was discharged was thin, reddish, and stank abominably. This was the Condition of this poor Woman, when we first applied our grand Dissolvent; the Pain she was attended with the first and second Day after was inconsiderable, nor did she complain of more afterwards, than would have been procured by the most mild and easy Remedy the Dispensatory affords. In four Days Time we found a very evident Alteration for the Better; for the Consistence of the Matter was changed, and the Surface of the *Cancerous Mass* became somewhat soft, we continued the Use of the same Medicine, and in a few Days more some part of the *Cancer* came away with the dressing. In short, in about six Weeks time, the whole Substance was entirely gone, and nothing remained to be done but to heal the Ulcer, which was effected in about a Fortnight. During the time she was under Cure we gave her a proper internal Medicine, not calculated to destroy the Acidity of the Blood, but to dispose the whole *Cancerous Mass*, with its Appendices to come away, which might otherwise, as the Seeds of the Disease, cause it to spring again: Thus was this Patient, (after so great a Fatigue she had undergone before she came to me) perfectly cured, and has continued so to this Time, without any manner of Inconvenience as she lately told me, it being a long time since she has been well.

A Gentlewoman near fifty Years of Age, by some Accident received a Blow on her left Breast, which in a few Days was succeeded by a considerable Tumour, whereupon she applyed herself to a *Surgeon*, who immediately let her Blood, ordered her to take the *Lap. Hibern.* in Posset-Drink, and embrocated the Breast with *Ol. Succini*: By the use of these Means the Swelling was much abated, a small Hardness only remaining, which did not exceed a small Wallnut in Bigness; in this State, with very little Pain, she continued above a Year; but being persuaded to apply an *Emp. de Ran. cum Mer.* to it, it encreased very apparently, was extreamly painful, and in Seven Months time became as big as a large Egg: After this she made use of a Woman who was reputed Famous for these Cases; but by One or Two of her Applications the Tumour became as big again as before: In short it continued to encrease gradually from that time, till the whole Breast, which was of a monstrous Bigness, and which was judged not to weigh less than Eight Pound, in time became entirely *Cancerous*. It was at this time that I saw it the Skin was very livid, looking sleek and shining, and seemed ready to open, as being scarce capable of longer containing such a prodigious hard *Mass* as laid concealed under it, and was in all Probability as big as the Breasts of the *Ammonian* Women, of which *Juvenal* thus speaks, *In Meroe, crasso majorem Infante Mamillam*. She had been with various experienced and reputable *Surgeons* before, among which was One not long ago deceased, who was justly looked upon as an Ornament of his Profession; but not one would willingly attempt a real Cure by cutting it off, or any other Way: They only prescribed some palliating Remedies to remove the Pain and prevent its Breaking. I was animated by my former Successes, and prevailed with my self to undertake it, not thinking I was at all blameable if my Success in so extraordinary an Affair contradicted the Prognosticks of so many worthy

Gentlemen; and though it did, I shall at all times think my self obliged to pay a Deference to them. I began the Cure by removing the Integuments from the upper Part of the Cancerous Substance, but did not wait for a Separation of the Slough the Escarotick made for fear of being incommoded in my Procedure by a Fungus; For this Reason I mixed some of our Dissolvent with a digestive Ointment, by which Means I had a Part of the *Cancerous Mass* came away with it, without any Trouble to my Patient. I continued this Method of Dressing several Days longer, with very little Alteration; but upon a Complaint of a Pain between the Shoulders, I was obliged to change my Medicine, and foment the *Cancer* with an Infusion of some of those Herbs that contain many *Volatile* attenuating and active Particles. And here I cannot but remark, by the by, that Applications to the pained Part would have been of no Effect, as I have many times observed, and particularly in a Woman which had a Cancerated Breast, that was violently afflicted with a Pain in her Arm on the same Side, which would not be removed by any of the Applications the Person that had the Care of her made use of the affected Arm. To this I might subjoin a very pertinent Case from *Galen*; but I fear I shall digress too far. The Pain of my Patient's Back being removed, I proceeded to apply the Dissolvent, which so softened the Superficies of the *Cancerous Mass* that in Three or Four Days Time I could take off above a Quarter of a Pound of it with the Edge or Back of my Incision Knife, and my Patient not so much as feel me, this I continued to accustom my self to, because it would have been more tedious to have waited for the coming away of the *Cancerous Mass* of it self. Sometimes I varied my Applications as I saw Occasion, but, as my Patient confessed, I scarce put her to any more Pain during the Time her Breast was dissolving (abating for the Pain of her Back) than there is in the dressing of an Issue. The prodigious Bigness of the *Cancerous Mass* made the Cure the more tedious, for it was above Three Months before all of it was entirely dissolved and gone; but this being at length surprisingly and very happily effected the *Cancerous Ulcer* (the last Part of the *Cancer* that came away left) was incarned and cicatrized by an Infusion of vulnerary Herbs, to which was added a small Quantity of Tincture of Myrrh: Thus was this Cure entirely compleated and my Success in it confirmed that *French* Proverb, which says, *It is better to be condemned to die by the Doctor, than by the Judge.* I did not make use of that internal Medicine I mentioned in the former Case, because here I found no pressing Necessity for the Use of it, but some other proper Physick was taken to dispose the Ulcer to heal, as one would have done in any other Case. Upon the whole of this Cure, I cannot say whether I had more Trouble with the *Cancer*, or in endeavouring to oblige my Patient to a strict Observance of some of the Non-Naturals she so often erred in. There is nothing can create a greater Trouble to the *Surgeon*, than to find Patients negligent of their Healths, by not endeavouring to prevent or regulate Miscarriages, nor taking so much Care of themselves, as they expect the *Surgeon* should take of them. The Rules and Directions of *Physicians* and *Surgeons*, given to their Patients, we have Reason to believe were not so often violated formerly; for in some Places they obliged themselves very strictly to the Observance of them, and some Historians give us an Account that *Selucus* made a Law; that if any of the *Epizephyrian Locrians* drank Wine, contrary to the *Physician*'s Direction, though they escaped the ill Consequents that might have attended it, Death was their Punishment, because they did contrary to what was prescribed them.

A Woman about Thirty Years of Age had been for a considerable Time afflicted with a hard painful Tumour under her Tongue, for the Cure of which she had applied her self to various Persons, but without Success. When I saw her I found the Swelling to be hard, painful, of a livid Appearance, and incommoded her so much in speaking, that she could not pronounce her Words articulately. I was of the Opinion of some Gentlemen that had seen it before me, *viz.* That it was undoubtedly *Cancerous*, and as such I proceeded to cure it; but I met with more Difficulties in this Case than I at first expected, for after I thought the *Cancerous Substance* had been entirely dissolved, and I had reduced the Ulcer to a very narrow Compass, it began to swell again, and in a short Time enlarged it self to almost the Bigness it was at first: This put me upon a Necessity of making an Incision into the Body of the Tumour, that I might commodiously come at the remaining Part, and so dispose some little Dossels of Lint, armed with our Dissolvent, that they might have their desired Effect, and this in every Respect answered what we proposed; so that we proceeded immediately to incarn the Ulcer, which we did by a Lotion prepared of an Infusion of some vulnerary Herbs, and *Mel. Rosar.* Thus was this Woman perfectly cured, and has continued well about a Year.

Because I have always found greater Difficulty in treating *Cancers* of the Mouth and Lips than those of the Breast, I will here relate an Instance of one upon the lower Lip that proved extreamly troublesome. It sometimes happens that one, or more, of those Glands which are spread on the Inside of the

Cheeks and Lips, called *Buccales* and *Labiales*, receive some Damage by a Bite or Blow; upon which they generally tumefy very much, become painful, and in Process of Time (if proper Means are not made use of) may become *Cancerous*. Such was the Case of a Woman about Thirty Years of Age, who having had a Blow on her lower Lip, neglected it till it was considerably tumefied, grew very painful, and became extreamly troublesome to her. The Circumference of the Swelling when I saw it, which was many Months after the Blow was received, was very much inflamed, and a small Quantity of *Icorous* Matter discharged from several small Pustules, which over-spread it; the Middle, which was the Body of the *Cancer*, was hard, of a whitish Colour, and moveable; it's Sides being only connected to the contiguous Parts by some small Filaments that were detached from it. The same Thing Doctor *Gendron* has discovered in an ulcerated *Cancer* on the Forehead of the Servant of a certain *Marquess*, as he observes in his Third *Chapter* of the Tract we have before mentioned. I began with my Patient by applying cool and temperate Remedies, till the Inflammation was considerably abated; after this I applied our Dissolvent, which operated so mildly that my Patient was not sensible of near so much Pain as before she was apprehensive of: In short, the Body of the *Cancer* was removed and a good digested Matter discharged from the Sore. Now all the Difficulty was after what Manner we should proceed to dispose the little *Cancerous* Branches in the Skin to come away, but this we effected after the following Manner; the Consistent of the Medicine we before applyed, was such as was no way qualified for rooting out the Cancerous Filaments, whereupon we were obliged to procure it's Dissolution in a proper Menstruum, though it required a considerable Time to do it; by this means, we soon found, that what before was ineffectual was now capable of effecting what we desired. This being done, the Ulcer was incarned by a Sarcotick Infusion (for I never use Ointments in these Cases) and cicatrized by the common drying Plaisters. It is to be observed, that the Scar still continues hollow (it having been healed near Two Years) and not like those that are the Consequents of well ordered simple Ulcers.

The following Observation contains an Account of one that was cured of an incipient *Cancer* in her Breast, by Internals. I was the rather inclined to set down the whole Process of this Cure, because by these, or such like Medicines, Persons under the same Circumstances may perhaps be cured, though by some they may be thought incurable. The Case is this; A

Gentlewoman, Thirty Years of Age, of a thin spare Habit of Body, by some Accident received a Blow upon One of her Breasts, which put her to an immediate Pain, and that very acute; but it lessened upon her being let Blood, and the Application of a discutient Plaister: However, in a few Days, some of the glandulous Grains of the Breast became indurated, and in Process of Time, by their Increase, they were rendered painful. At this Time she sought out for fresh Advice, and continued Two Months under the Care of a Person she was recommended to; but Things not succeeding according to Expectation, she became a Patient to Three or Four more. During this Time the Lump continued to encrease but slowly, and at the Expiration of Six Months it appeared to be a very hard painful Tumour in the Middle of the Breast, but no bigger than a Hen-Egg; whereupon it was thought proper to commence her Method of Cure by exhibiting the following *Pills.* ℞ *Pill. Tartar. Quercetan.* ʒß. *Calomel* gr. viii. *F. Pill.* Nᵒ 5. These were likewise continued twice a Week during the whole Cure; after this, was ordered the following Infusion, ℞ *Vin. Rhenan.* ℔ii. *Milleped.* ʒii. *Ocul. Canc.* ʒß *Croci.* ʒii. This was not to be taken alone, but when it had stood Four and Twenty Hours, three or four Spoons-full of it was to be mixed with a Draught of the ensuing Dietetick-Drink, and taken in the Morning, and at Four of the Clock in the Afternoon. ℞ *Rad. Sarsaparill.* ʒii. *Chinæ* ʒvi. *Fig. Sassafr.* ʒi. *Corn. Cervi,* ʒ*Sem. Correand.* ʒß. *Sant. Rub.* ʒii. *Coq. in aq. Font. Congiis 4 per Horæ dimidium, deinde stent Clause super Cineres Calidos per Horas* xii; *postea ebulliant ad tertiæ Partis Consumptionem.* By the Continuance of these Means about two Months, and observing a regular Method of living, the Cure of this Patient was effected; though by some she had been looked upon as incurable, unless she would submit the cutting it out, which is not often attended with Success.

Perhaps, *Sir*, here you may object, that it is acting disengenuously, and not like a Friend, to give you an Account of those Persons only where I have succeeded. To this I answer, that excepting one Woman, that was emaciated almost to the last Degree by the excessive Discharge of a fætid Icorous Matter from her Breast, and an Abscess under her Arm, and who was carried off by a violent Loosness, I never had a Person miscarried under my Care, where I proposed a Cure. That poor Woman I suffered my self to be persuaded to take care of, having but little Prospect of effecting it, yet my Endeavours succeeded so well, that had it been in our Power to put a Stop to her

Loosness, I am of opinion she might have been cured.

What has been hitherto said, I do not question but is sufficient to satisfy you, that this formidable *Disease* is not so rebellious, but that it may be sometimes conquered by Art; and I might here relate a Case I have at this present Writing, wherein not only a Part of the *Cancer* was fixed, but there were hard *Cancerous* Knots extended to the Arm-pit; and yet this seems to be almost well; the Ulcer that remains, and which heals daily, not being much broader than a Crown Piece. But in regard the Patient is not entirely cured, I shall reserve this Relation untill another Opportunity; though I will embrace the present to assure you that I am,

SIR,

Your very respectful Brother,

and Humble Servant,

W^m. Beckett.

Hatton-Garden,
July 12, 171 .

A Solution of some Curious Problems *concerning* Cancers.

PROBLEM I.

Whether the Cancerous Juice is Corrosive, or not.

W E cannot come to a certain Knowledge of the Principles of the Juice which is lodged in the Cancerous Substance, although it enjoyed the very same Properties, of that which is discharged from an ulcerated *Cancer*, from the Account which Authors have given of the latter; for they have differed very much in determining the Nature of the Salts, with which they suppose it abounds. *Helmont, Van Horne,* and most of those Gentlemen that were Chymically inclined, were of Opinion they belonged to the Alkaline Family, but a far greater Number than those, have thought they are Acid. *Riolan,* the Father, in his Chirurgical Works, without giving his Opinion what the constituent Parts of the purulent Matter are, affirmed it to be as strong as Poison, and that no Death could be devised too cruel for such a One as should give it to a Man. This brings *Vide* Riolanus, *Cap.* 13. *Sect.* 2. to my Remembrance a very unhappy Accident a Gentleman informed me of that befel Mr *Smith,* one of the *Surgeons* of St *Thomas's Hospital,* who being so curious as to taste the Juice of a cancerated Breast presently after it was extirpated, found himself very strangely affected by it, in a very short Time; he washed his Mouth with various Things, but nothing could free him from that penetrating, malignant, and nauseous Savour, he was continually attended with; in short, he became consumptive, and in a few Months died a Martyr to the Art of *Surgery.* I confess when I received this Account it did not a little surprize me, because I had several times had the Curiosity to do the very same Thing, at the *Hospital* where that unfortunate Genman made the Experiment. I never found any remarkable Sharpness in it, though it was always attended with a very unpleasant Savour. I proceeded at first very cautiously in making this Attempt; for I deluted some Drops of the Juice in several Spoons-full of fair Water, till at length, not finding any Inconvenience from it, I came to the Juice it self. We cannot imagine the Death of that Gentleman beforementioned, was procured by the Action of any corrosive Salts, whether *Acid* or *Alkaline,* which would have caused a Corrosion of the Parts, but that it is only accountable from the extraordinary Stench and Malignity of the Matter, which impressing its Virulency on the Animal Juices must undoubtedly disturb their regular Motions, and cause the utmost Confusion of the whole Oeconomy. It must certainly be a very tragical Scene, to observe how Nature, by so inconsiderale Means, confounds and insults, over the Animal System; but still there is nothing we are more certain of, than that her Method of Procedure is always consistent to the Rules she acts by. Since the writing of this, looking over a little Tract which informs us of the Rarities in *New-England,* I met with a Relation which discovers to us the peculiar and odd Quality of the Juice of a cancerated Breast, or Wolf, as our Author calls it. He tells us that an indulgent Husband, by sucking his Wife's sore Breast to draw out the Poison, lost all his Teeth, but was attended by no other Inconvenience. Now this does not prove that so strange an Effect should succeed the sucking the Ulcer, because of the Corrosiveness of the Matter; for had it been so, such tender Parts as the Gums, Lips, and Tongue, could not have escaped so well as to have received no Damage by it.

Problem II.

Whether Cancers *are contagious, or not.*

THERE has been a very great Disagreement in the Sentiments of our Predecessors as to this Point; but *Zacutas Lusitanus* proposes to prove it by Reason and Experience. His Reasons are, *First*, because in an ulcerated

Vid. *Zacut. de Prax.* Med. admirand. *Lib.* 1. *Obs.* 15.

Cancer there is a Cadaverous Stench and Rottenness, which infects the Neighbouring Parts with it's Virulency. *Secondly*, Because a *Cancer* is the same *Disease* as an *Elephantiasis*, and *Leprosy* of a particular Part. To this, *Sennertus* in his Posthumous Works answers, that all corrupted and fætid

Substances are not contagious; for in a *Gangrene* and *Sphacellus*, there is the greatest Corruption and offensive Smell, yet we do not find that a Person is killed by it: He adds, though a *Cancer* has some Similitude to an *Elephantiasis*, they are different *Diseases*. *Lusitanus* deduces his Experience from an Observation of a poor Woman, that having an ulcerated *Cancer* in her Breast, and lying with three Children, they were affected after the same Manner by the Contagion. He says that Two of them died, but the Third, which was of a stronger Constitution, had the *Cancer* cut off by a *Surgeon* and was cured. *Sennertus* is of Opinion that these Children did not contract the *Disease* by Contagion, but that it was by Hereditary Succession. We likewise find that *Cardan*, *Lib. de Venen. Cap.* 12. is of Opinion that *Cancers* are not

Vid Sennert. *Paralipom. ad Part.* 1 Cap. 19.

contagious. However, we will not make any particular Enquiry into these Authors Reasons, when they so strenuously maintain this Point; but only relate a remarkable History, which will prove the contrary, if the *Cancerous* Matter comes to an immediate Contract with a soft and glandulous Part. The Relation I had (some time ago) from a Gentleman not long since deceased, who, out of a pious Disposition, had devoted himself for several Years last past, to be serviceable to the greatest Objects of Charity. He informed me that a Tradesman's Wife in *Nottingham*, being so unhappy as to labour under a *Cancer* in one of her Breasts, her Husband was of Opinion he could relieve her by sucking it; accordingly he put this Method in Practice, in hopes without doubt he could effect a Cure, by drawing the *Cancerous* Matter out of the Nipple; he continued his Attempts for some Time, but found it did not answer his Design; for though a small Quantity of Matter was discharged this way, the *Disease* still became worse, and she terminated her Life soon after. Two Months were scarce expired before the Husband of the Deceased came up to *London*, upon Account of a swelling he had arose on the Inside of the upper Jaw; he applied himself to some ingenious *Surgeons* for Advice, who assured him he must undergo the drawing of Several Teeth on that Side of the Jaw which was affected, and have the Swelling, and Part of the Jaw-Bone (if necessary) cut away; he went away very much disatisfyed with so harsh a Proposal, and became a Patient to a Person, who undertook to cure him with *Gargels*, and such inconsiderable Remedies; however, by the Use of these Things he was of Opinion he became much better, and thought he should be cured. Upon this he retired into the Country to his Business, but in less than a Month's Time he was obliged to come up again, and have the former Method put in Practice. But the Event was according to that Expression of *Galen*, *Quibus item sunt Cancri in cavitate Corporis, aut Palato, sede utero, si secentur, aut urantur, ulcera cicatrice induci non possunt.* For the Sore could never be brought to cicatrize, but the *Cancer* continu'd to spread, till it had extended in self over most of the internal Parts of the Mouth, and to the inner Part of the Nose: In this unhappy Condition, he lived some time, but at last became so frightful an Object, and the Stench that continually proceeded from the Parts was so offensive, that he retired himself from the World, and finished his miserable Life in a Garret. Since the finishing the *Solution* to the foregoing *Problem*, I met with a Surgeon (a Foreigner) who giving me an Account of the present State of the Practice of *Surgery* in the Country where he lived, and relating some considerable Cases which had happened within his own Knowledge, in answer to my Desire, among other things, told me, without any particular Intimation from me, he knew a very odd Accident, which happened upon a Woman's having an ulcerated *Cancer* in her right Breast, which was, that she being poor, for want of other Conveniences, suffered two Children she had to lie with her in that Condition; at length one of them, a Girl about five Years old, began to be afflicted with a small painful Tumour in one of her Breasts, which encreasing to near the Bigness of an Egg, became Livid, and entirely *Cancerous*; the Mother died some time after,

Vide Galen. *in* Aph. Hip. Com. Lib. 6 Aph. 38.

and the Child did not long survive her; but the other Child continued well. Several Surgeons gave their Sentiments of this Case; some thought it to be an Hereditary Indisposition; but considering the Mother had no Appearance of a *Cancer* before or at the Birth of the Child, I cannot but readily embrace the Opinion of those Gentlemen, that were inclined to believe that it was contracted by Contagion, seeing the Position of the Child's Body was such in Bed, that that Part of it which was affected was almost always disposed to rub against the Dressings soaked in Matter, (for I understand the Mother took but very little Care to change them often.) Now it is not at all probable, that the malignant *Effluvia*, which continually pass off from the *Cancerous Mass*, and the putrefied Matter, can dispose a Person at any little Distance to be affected with the like *Disease*, for then the other Child would have became a Sufferer; but it may happen in some extraordinary Cases, where the corrupted Fluid has attained an exalted Pitch of Malignity, to communicate some of its more active Particles to the Blood and Spirit; and so causing a very great Disorder in their Motions produce a violent Fever, and Confusion of the whole Oeconomy, so as to occasion a Person's Death. But see a remarkable Case in *Tulpius, Lib.* 4. *Obs.* 8. That there are several cutaneous *Diseases* that may be propagated by Contagion, if a Person lies with another, is by all allowed of; and that the lying with a Person that has a *Cancer* may be attended by such a *Disease*, from the Proofs we have brought, I suppose will be agreed to be equally as certain. But this cannot happen unless the matter be very malignant, and be suffered, by the Negligence of the Patient, to come to an immediate Contact, with a Part of the Body of the other Person; for then, without doubt, it may contuminate the Fluids, and incline them to assume a Viscidity, to which the *Effluvia* will immediately adhere, because they are best qualifyed for a Union with those Substances that are viscous. To this we may add, that in those Persons that are nearly related, the Malignity may be more easily communicable because of their Analogy to each other; for consonant hereto, *Diemerbroeck* says in his Treatise of *the Plague*, that *Kindred more easily receive the Infection from one another.* But see more in that Author's excellent Book where you have likewise some curious Thoughts relating to Contagion.

Vide *Diemer-broeck* de *Pest.* Page 58.

PROBLEM III.

Whether if the extirpating a Cancerous Breast *happens to be*

*successful, it ought to be look'd upon as a Consequence of
Performing the Operation better than our Predecessors.*

B Y the Account we receive from Authors we cannot be positively assured, whether there was any particular established Method in the first Ages of this Art, for the Performance of this Operation: This we are only assured of that there are some Circumstances which relate to it, that have been taken Notice of; the most considerable of which is, that the actual Cautery was to be applied immediately after the Abscision; this they advised, not only to put a Stop to the Flux Vide *Ætius Tetrab.* 4. Ser. 4. *Cap.* 44. of Blood, but likewise to correct the ill Quality of it: It is to be observed, that they ordered always, upon such an Occasion, Defensatives to be applied to the contiguous Parts, to prevent their being inflamed; but for as much as they were sensible the actual Cautery would procure an Eschar, they recommended the Use of Digestives to separate it; after which, they proposed to heal it as a common Ulcer. The very next Advance this Operation received, that we have met with, was by that Accurate Writer *Franciscus Arceus,* who obliged the World with an exact and methodical Account of the whole Method of Procedure in extirpating a Cancer in the Breast; though this Author would only venture on Vide *Arceus,* lib. 2. Cap 3. de *Curand. Vulnerib.* those that were not Ulcerated, those that were he looked upon as incurable. We do not find that this Method was recommended to the World by any remarkable Histories of Cures effected by it; whether it proceeded from the Unsuccessfulness of the Attempts, or its Disuse, we cannot determine. *Fabritius Hildanus* likewise made a considerable Step towards the Encouraging the Performing this Operation; and he assures us, he has more than once done it with Success; he did not only influence his Cotemporaries to revive an Operation, that was, perhaps, almost grown out of Date, by the Histories of some Cases he recites; but obliged them with the Figure of a Pair of Forceps, which in this Operation are very convenient to engage the Breast, and thereby prevent the Pain the Patients are sometimes put to, by piercing the Breast with Needles armed with Silk to suspend it. There are several Ways of performing the Operation, mentioned by later Practitioners, but at this Time there are few that are willing to be concerned in it. A very considerable Author speaking of extirpating a *Cancerous Breast,* advises us to take care we do not cut the Pectoral Muscle in the Operation: But we have seen a very remarkable Case of this Nature, where a Part of that Muscle was cut away, and the Cartilages of the two of the Ribs laid bare, and the Patient happened to be cured. Now if our Predecessors had so great a Respect to the avoiding the wounding of this Part, as to make their Incisions too superficial, their Operations must be in all Probability unsuccessful; for we are very well assured by Experience, that their actual Cauteries will have no good Effect here, nor will they consume the remaining Part of the *Cancerous Mass*. We have elsewhere shewed, that this Substance upon boiling becomes hard and friable; and we will here take the Liberty to give our Opinion of the Use of Cauteries in this Case. The *Cancerous Substance* we take to be nothing more than a Transformation of the small glandulous Bodies, which form the Breast, and a Lymphatick Juice, intimately incorporated therewith, into a hard, close, whitish, and (by common Medicines) indissolvable *Mass*. In some Cases, perhaps, it may receive some Addition from some Juices, which may distil from the contiguous Fibres. This being granted, what Benefit, can we reasonably imagine, will ensue on this painful Method? Will not the Fire, by causing the more Fluid Parts of the *Mass* to evaporate, actually dry up, torrefy, and harden it; and so dispose it for displaying a Train of mischievous Effects, on the contiguous Parts? and all this without any very apparent Decrease of it too: Nay, the very reducing of it to such a Consistence, which very much resembles a Piece of burnt Horn, is sufficient to procure a perpetual Pain, seeing Medicines can hardly soften it, so as to reduce it to its first State.

PROBLEM IV.

Whether Salivation *will Cure a* Cancer.

T H E extraordinary Success this Method has been attended with, in some Cases of the greatest Difficulty, has so far recommended it to the World, that it is at this Time become of so great Repute, that there are few Persons but what will willingly embrace it, if proposed to them, provided they have found former Methods prove ineffectual. We once knew a Person, who laboured under an ulcerated *Cancer* in her Breast, advised to it, and who had certainly under-gone it, though contrary to the Opinion of some Persons concerned, if in three or four Days time she had not been reduced to such a weak Condition, that it put an End to the Controversy. That a *Salivation* has cured the most malign and spreading Ulcers, and those that have been of several

Years continuance, notwithstanding their Edges have been high, inverted and assumed the Consistence of a callous Body, we have found by several Instances; but that it should cure a *Cancerous Ulcer*, an *Ulcer* which is chiefly seated in a transformed animal Substance, and which has no Correspondence with the contiguous Parts, is what we cannot believe. One of the principal Effects of *Mercury*, if prudently given, is, that it attenuates the Juices, clears the Canals, destroys the ill Quality of that Fluid that has a Hand in causing any Obstruction, and renders the Juices temperate and sweet. By effecting this, it is, that it cures so many different Diseases, which perhaps have not so great a Diversity in their Causes, but have different Appearances, which depend upon the Variety of Parts, where the Cause operates. From hence any One may judge, that a Person who discovers a certain Method of curing *Cancers* by Medicines only, will find that it will not consist in a Secret for purifying the Juices, which can have no Effect on the *Cancerous Mass*, so as to procure it's Dissolution; and without a Remedy for which his Method will be always unsuccessful. *Mercklin*, in his Treatise *de Transfus Sanguinis*, page 35, tells us we have no Reason to believe we may have Success from Transfusion in a *Cancer*, nor indeed would Injections succeed better; though, perhaps, by this Means, it is possible so to alter the Fluids, that *Ulcers*, not *Cancerous*, may be cured in a short Time, as it once happened to a certain Person, who being under Cure for an inveterate Pox, had some *Rosin* of *Scammony* infused in the Essence of *Guaiacum*, injected into his Veins, which Vomited him excessively; but his *Ulcers* were healed in three Days Time. From what has been hitherto said, it is evident, that a *Salivation* can never cure a confirmed *Cancer*, because it is not capable of procuring a Dissolution of that hard Substance, which is the real *Cancer* it self. The Glands we have observed, with the extravasated *Lympha*, and its Vessels, are perfectly changed to a different Substance to what they were before, all which make a *Mass* of such a Nature, that it will be impossible to procure it's Dissolution by any inward Means. If the *Cancer* was nothing more than a Coagulation of the Juices in the Vessels, or other Canals, or Pipes, the Cure might be much more easily effected, but as the *Cancer* is conjoined with such Circumstances as we have mentioned, we may affirm the Cure will be altogether impossible without the whole Substance with it's Appendices or Branches (which we have found they often have) be taken away; or a perfect Dissolution of all of it be procured by some external Remedy, which is capable of operating on it after such a peculiar Manner, as to dissolve the *Cancerous Substance*, without having any such Effect on the contiguous Parts.

PROBLEM V.

Whether Cancers are Curable by Causticks.

THE Difficulty that those of our Predecessors who had Courage enough to attempt the Cure of *Cancers*, must unavoidably meet with, obliged them to enter upon several Methods of Practice, in order to be capable of surmounting it; and there have not been wanting for these several hundred Years last past, some Gentlemen in the Republick of Medicine that have proposed to conquer this Rebellious Disease, by the use of some particular Causticks, they have recommended. It is foreign to my Design, to give an Account of the Composition of the several Remedies, they have been big with the Expectation of Success from; I shall only take notice of one or two not very pompous Preparations, that by some Persons I know, have been looked upon as extraordinary as any that have been transmitted to us. *Guido*, who I think I may justly say is one of the best Authors of so ancient a Date, has been very lavish of his Encomiums on *Arsnick*, and after him *Fallopius, Rodericus a Castro, Ossenius, Penotus, Faber, Borellus*, and others, have recommended it in some particular Preparations. That of *Fuschius*, who is said to have cured abundance of Persons of *Cancers*, in *England, Germany*, and *Poland*, having had the most said in it's Commendation, required our more particular Notice; *Hartman* calls it *Pul Benedictus*, which whether it deserves that Title, we will leave to the Reader to judge, after we have faithfully recounted the Effects of it. Its Preparation is as follows: ℞ *Arsenici albi ʒi subtilissime pulverisetur per dies 15 de die tertio in tertium affundatur Aq. vitæ, ut cooperiat pulverem, post triduum Aq. vitæ abjiciatur, ac nova affundatur, ac misceantur. Rad Dracunouli Major, mense julio vel Agu. collect & in taleolas scissæ ac in loco ventis perflatili exsiccatæ ʒii. Fuliginis Camini splendidi ʒiii redigantur omnia in subtilissimum pulverem super lapidem marmoreum, & servetur in Vase bene clauso vitreo. Ante annum vero ad usum non erit it a commodus.* This Powder I applied to a *Cancered* Breast of a Woman, under thirty Years of Age, after having made a Sore by applying one of the milder *Causticks*; the first Night it was made use of, it caused a great deal of pain, and the next Day, the Breast appeared very much tumefied and inflamed, a small quantity of Gleet, having discharged on the Bolster: in short for fifteen Days she was not free from pain, she had a *Fever*, was attended with frequent *Vomitings*, *Faintings*, and several other Disorders. I could afford her but very little Relief by Internals, or the most cool and temperate Applications to the Breast; nor was it in my Power to remove the dressing, it adhered so fast to the Sore. There was a Discharge of a bloody ferous Juice for twelve Days in a moderate quantity, after which the Matter thickened, and it began to smell somewhat offensive, at the end of fifteen Days the Dressing dropped off, and with it came away about two Ounces of the *cancerous Mass*. The Reader may easily imagine that making so small a Progress in such a time, and that at the Expence of so much Pain, I could easily prevail with my self to desist from the Undertaking, for the second Application would have been attended with the same Inconveniencies as the first, which to any Persons that entertains such a concern for his Patients as he ought to do, must be very fatiguing; in short, after this I made use of that Remedy I had elsewhere mentioned, and which from its Effect was properly enough called a *Dissolvent*, with this by the Blessing of God the *Cancerous* Substance was consumed in about three Weeks, and a perfect Cure compleated in not many Days after, the Patient which I saw lately continuing perfectly well, it being the first Case that ever Providence directed me to the use of the Remedy in. *Hildan* has an Observation very pertinent to what we have before related; he tells us, that the *Powder* so much celebrated by *Penotus*, and which is much the same with that just now mentioned, being applied to a *Cancer*, was succeeded by such ill Symptoms, that it killed the Patient in a few Days. We are informed in the communicated Observations of *Riverius*, that a Foreigner extirpated a Cancer, that had began to Ulcerate in the Breast of a Woman of fifty Years of Age, by the following Application: ℞ *Arsenici* ℈i. *Salis Armoniaci* ℥ii. *Sublimat. crud.* ℥iiii. *Aq; Fortis* ℥i. *These were to be distill'd to Dryness, then an equal Weight of distill'd Vinegar put thereto, which was to be distilled again, till the remaining Matter, became of the Consistance of a Paste.* The Surgeon bathed the *Cancer* with hot Wine, and rubbed it with Cloths for some time to *irritate* it, then he spread some of his Composition on a Bolster six times less than the *Tumour*, and applied it; in twenty four Hours time, it made an *Escar* as large as the Swelling, so that it wholly consumed the *Cancer*; after the Separation of the *Escar* he incarned the *Ulcer* and cicatrized it. It is very observable, that he did not engage in this painful Process, without immediately causing a Fever, which was attended with a *Vomiting, Loosness*, and much Provocation of *Urine*; which Symptoms lasted two or three Days, for Nature was disordered by the destructive Quality of a venemous Remedy. *Paracelsus*, *Faber*, and some others, make mention of Arsnical Preparations, that procure but little Pain in their Operation; I had a Design of making a Trial of some of these Remedies, had I not in my Enquiries met with what was very satisfactory to me, though after knowing what I have related, I should have always cautiously avoided the use of any Remedy, in which the *Arsnick* had not undergone such a Preparation as I should have approved of, because I am assured it may procure very mischievious Symptoms, though in Substance, it do not so much as touch the Skin, witness the *Amulets*, in which it has been the chief Ingredient, and of which there have been such direful Accidents related by *Crato*, *Massaria*, and *Zacutus Lucitanus*. I do not think it impossible, but that *Arsnick* may be prepared after such a manner as may, by the addition of some convenient Body, or depriving it of its noxious Particles, qualify it for effecting uncommon things in the Cure of this Disease, without causing the Surgeon to repent the use of it. I remember that *Helmont* somewhere says one may easily enough correct several sorts of Poisons, so that they shall not be deprived of their Force, when we destroy their Virulency. Many Instances of this Nature we meet with in Mr *Boyle*, and some others; but that which makes most for my present purpose, is, what is mentioned by the last Honourable Gentleman, of a very ingenious Man he knew, that was famous, as well for his Writings, as for a Remedy to cure *ulcerated Cancers* in Womens Breasts, without any considerable Pain. He assured our Author that his Medicine was indolent, and mortified the ulcerated Parts as far as they were corrupted, without disordering the Party, and this Remedy it seems partly by the Confession of the Gentleman, was reasonably enough supposed to be a Dulcification of *Arsnick*; one would think that the mention of this very Remedy, with Monsieur *Alliot's*, and that recommended in the preceeding Letter, should be sufficient to influence the inquisitive of our Profession to farther Enquiries, which must be certainly an Undertaking, worthy the noblest Spirits. To conclude, we cannot say, but there are many Cancers that may be cured by Causticks, but the Person that is to undergo it, may very well answer, as a certain Patient did, who's Thigh was to be cut off, *Non est tanto digna dolore Salus. The Preservation of Life would be too dear bought at the Price of so much Pain.* This puts me in Mind of what is related of *Galienus* the Emperor, who it seems had for a considerable time been very grieviously afflicted with a *Sciatica*, a certain Physician undertaking to cure him, performed indeed his Promise, but nevertheless made him undergo a thousand painful Experiments; whereupon, the Emperor one Day sent for, and thus said to him, *Take* Fabatus *two Thousand Sesterces, but withal, be informed I give them not for curing my* Sciatica, *but that thou may'st never cure me again.*

PROBLEM VI.

Whether Cancers are Curable by internal Medicines.

THOUGH this *Problem* at first View may seem to be too near allied to that which proves the Impossibility of curing cancerous Tumours, whether ulcerated or not, by Salivation; yet in regard there are some Persons, that tell us the Disease is superable by some internal Remedies, which operate after a quite different Manner, to those generally given to procure a Salivation, we shall enquire into one of the most considerable of them, related by a Person whose Memory we have a very great Value for. And we shall the rather take Notice of this particular Remedy, because we have elsewhere spoke of the Success of it. It were no very difficult Matter for me to mention several internal Medicines, out of our Chirurgical Writers, more especially those that have been Favourers of Chemistry; but I shall purposely decline it, because to speak freely, I suspect that most of the Remedies, though much has been said in the Praise, have not been sufficiently examined by those that recommended them. To this we may add, that had the Authors of them considered the vast Difference there is to be observed in Cancers, they would not have so suddainly and positively determined, that their Medicines were of use in these Cases in general; seeing we must have regard to absolutely different Intentions, in those that are not ulcerated, and those that are, and those that are a hard Tumour, and those that are flat, and likewise when they are conjoined with Circumstances, which are often enough to be met with. The Honourable Mr *Boyle* in his *Usefulness of experimental Philosophy*, tells us, that he was informed by credible Persons, of a certain *English* Woman above sixty Years of Age, who had lain long indisposed with a Cancer in her Breast, in an Hospital in *Zeeland*, and was by Doctor *Harberfeld*, with one single inward Remedy perfectly cured in three Weeks; the Relation was made by a *Doctor of Physick*, who was an Eye Witness of the Cure, and another Person who not only saw the Cure, but knew the Woman before, and out of Charity, carried her to him that healed her. Our Author was informed, that the *Chemical*

Liquor the Doctor constantly made use of, does in the Dose of about a Spoonful or two, work suddainly and nimbly enough by Vomit, but hath very quickly ended it's Operation, so that within an Hour, or less, after the Patient has taken it, he is commonly well again, and very hungry. He adds, that having some of the Liquor presented him, he found the Taste to be offensive enough, and not unlike that of *Vitriol*, which by the Taste and emetick Operation, was guessed to be it's principal Ingredient. The Relators assured our Author they had been in *England*, as well as elsewhere partly Eye Witnesses, and partly Performers of wonderful Cures by the help of it alone, under God, in the *King's Evil*; insomuch, that an eminent Gentleman of this Nation, hath been cured by it, when *that Distemper* had brought his Arm to such a pass, that the Surgeons had appointed a time to cut it off. Now, who is there, that upon reading this Account would not think the Doctor a very happy Man, that was Master of so valuable a Secret; but alas! How satisfactory would it be to the World if the hundredth part of the Remedies that have been handed down to us, had a Power of effecting those things that are ascribed to them, without being attended with any ill Consequences. I assure you, Reader, I have made use of this very Remedy, for since I mentioned it as the Doctor's having great Success from it; I met with the true Preparation of it, as it was communicated to Sir *Kenelm Digby* by Doctor *Havervelt*, or *Haberfield*, for the Cure of *Cancers*, the *King's Evil*, and old *Ulcers*. It is as follows. ℞ *Dantzick Vitriol, calcine it till it be yellow, then grind it with Salt, or Salt Petre, the ordinary proportion with this Sublime Mercury, which Sublime once again by it self, then take only the Cristaline part of it; of this take ℥i, grind it to a Subtile Powder in a Glass Mortar with a Glass Pestle.* Put this into a Glass Bottle, and pour upon it a Quart of Fountain Water, stop the Bottle close, and let it stand thus for some Days, shaking it often; after it is well settled pour off the clear, and filtre it; take a Spoonful of this Liquor, which put into a Vial, and put to it two Spoonfuls of fair Water; shake the Vial well, and let the Patient Drink it in the Morning Fasting: As to the quickness of its Operation, and the making the Patient Hungry, I found it at first to agree with what Mr *Boyle* says of it; but upon giving it three or four times, the Patient would afterward complain of a Languidness, which was ushered in by a Sickness at the Stomach; after this, they would be attended with a Heat or Soreness of the Throat, immoderate Thirst, convulsive Motions of the Stomach, &c. Some of which Inconveniencies would continue for many Hours together. It was upon Account of the Melancholy Reflections of bringing the Patients into such Disorder, and their Unwillingness to endure such Fatigues, that I had never Courage enough to proceed in this Method. I cannot but say, upon the Alteration I found in a Patient of mine, from the use of six Doses of this Medicine, that it may as well as some other churlish Remedies, cure some flat ulcerated Cancers, where there is no Tumour to dissolve, in Persons that are capable of often repeating it, which I think is sufficient to put us upon farther Enquiries, that we may be able to accomplish such Undertakings without bringing upon the Patient such a Train of mischievous Accidents.

POSTSCRIPT.

What follows is taken from a Manuscript which at this time 1714–15, belongs to one of the Family of the *Pains*, that have for a long time pretended to cure Cancers: In the Margin is this Note, (*Used by my Father, and Grandfather, and Brothers, and known as a thing excellent by long Practice in our Family of the* Pains:) The Book was lent me by my Brother *Dobyns*, who had it from one of the Family, a Patient of his.

The Red Caustick.

To eat all Superfluous Cancerous and Schirrous Matters gathered hard in the Edges or Sides of any Ulcer or Cancer, breeding upon the Mouth, Face, Nose or Valva. Take of Bole Armoniac one Ounce, of yellow Arsnic three Ounces, powder them and searse them fine, pare an Apple or two and take of the Pulp and put so much of it to the Powder (beating of it together in a Mortar) as will make it of the stiffness of Dough, then make it up into round Balls of the bigness of a Walnut, dry them in a Chamber-Window till they be hard enough. When you use these Balls shave a little off from them into your Hand, and moisten the same with a little Spittle, and rub it well about the hard Foot of the *Noli me Tangere*, and all over the Head of the same, and after that you have gathered him up into the Ligature and knit him hard up (for it seems they used a Ligature smeared with the Medicine) then apply your Preparation before-mentioned, and lay fine Holland Raggs dipt in the following Red Water, all over the said Caustic, and so let it lye till it fall off its self. *Note*, The Quantity of Caustic laid on, ought not to be much, and yet sufficient to work its effect. It worketh with great Pain for twelve Hours or more, and after that by Fits, like the Tooth-Ach; as the Pain worketh off it causes great Inflammation and Swelling about those Parts it is applied to, but this does not continue above four or five Days; so meddle not with it till the Caustick comes off. Then you may for three or four Days dress the Inflammation with Diachylon Plaister, or the Red Water warm.

The Red Water for a Cancer.

Quench unslacked Lime in boiling Water, which let stand six Hours, the clear Water poured off, put to the Fire again; to a Gallon and half of which, put *Camphir* ℥ß *Aloes Succatrine* ℥ß. *Common Bole* ℥ii *White Copperas or Allum* ℥ii all powdered, which boil in the Liquor a little while: He sometimes gave a Pill made of Deflograted Red Precipitate, which sometimes made them spit a little.

The Musilage Plaister to dissolve Schirrous Knots in the Breast.

Take of the white and inward Bark of the Witch-Hasel half a Handful, cut it short and stamp it, then take of the Roots of Marsh Mallows, Holy-hock Roots two or three Roots, clean them and throw away the Pith, stamp all together, then take of Fenugreek and Linseed of each two Ounces powdered, put all in an Earthen-pot, then take a Pint of white Wine or Water, heat it scalding hot, put it to the Things aforesaid, cover it close, stirring it every Day for nine Days, then strain out the Musilage Liquor with which you make the following Plaister. Take a Pint of Salad Oyl, Cerus finely powdered 8 Ounces, boil them together, constantly stirring them, a sufficient time, which you may know by its coming clear off a Pewter Dish when dropt on, let it cool a little and put in your Musilage, which stir till it be as white as you would have it, and until almost all the Musilage be boiled away, then remove it from the Fire and put to it four Ounces of *yellow Wax*, probably *Galbanum* may be better, which when dissolved and the Plaister cold, work up for use. This Plaister is sometimes used with equal Parts of *Galbanum*.

THE

CASE

OF

Dr *JAMES KEIL,*

Represented by

JOHN RUSHWORTH.

I Should not have been induced to make these Papers publick, barely on account of the rash Censures, that are frequently cast upon the Practice of *Surgery*, not attended with Success; tho' that Consideration alone, in the Case of a Person of such Value and Eminency in *Physick*, as Dr K E I L is known to have been, may be thought sufficient to have moved me to it: But being certainly informed, That several *Physicians* and *Surgeons* have before, and since his Death, given themselves the Liberty to reflect, not only upon me for Using, but also upon the Deceased for submitting to the Methods that were taken with him; I think I shall not discharge my Duty, either to my Friend, or to my Self, or indeed to the Profession, if I do not, as far as I am able, endeavour to set what was done in a True Light.

In order thereunto, it may be requisite to look back to the Time He first mentioned any Disorder in his Mouth to me, which was in *August* 1716. He then told me, He had preceived a Fulness in his Mouth for very many Years; but in the last Three or Four Years it was much encreased, and by the Bulk began to be troublesome to him, tho' not in the least painful: Upon examining it, I found the Tumour not only large, but also to fluctuate, and therefore told him, until I was satisfied what was contained in it, I could not come to a Resolution, as to the manner of treating it; but, if he pleased, I would make an Incision into it, and then would tell him what I thought was fit to be done; He was very well satisfied, and resolved I should proceed accordingly.

Upon Opening it, there appeared to be nothing contained in it, but Blood; not in the least altered in Colour, Consistence, or Smell, from what is contained in the Vessels. The Tumour presently sunk very much, and I dilated the Incision with my Probe-Scissers, and pressed in some *Dossels*; and then told him, it was a fleshy Tumour, called a *Sarcoma*, and that the Blood contained in it was only accidental; and that the best way of extirpating it was by the actual *Cautery*; but I let him know, that I feared it would be more troublesome to him, and take longer Time to cure, than he seemed to expect.

We presently sent for the best *Instrument-Maker* the Country afforded, and gave him Directions: But that Night: talking with him of his Case, I desired him to consider, Whether it might not be thought a Slight, by the Learned of both Professions, if I should Perform the Operation, upon a Man of his Character, without a Consultation; there being no Reason (but the Loss of his Time) to be in haste. At first he seemed unwilling to lose so much Time, yet upon Consideration, he resolved for *London* the next Day, where several *Physicians* and *Surgeons* were consulted; they all agreed, it was a simple *Sarcoma*, and that the actual *Cautery* was the properest, if not the only means of curing it. This Account I received from the Doctor by Letter; as also, that the *Surgeons*, upon probing, found the Bone bare, and from the ill Smell concluded it was foul: "Which, said the Doctor it was impossible for you to discover; because after I left *Northampton*, Two *Dossels* of the first Dressing dropt out." I was very glad to hear That, for those *Dossels* lodging so long, in that warm Part, I was in hopes might be the Occasion of the fœtid Smell; which the *Surgeons*, not being acquainted with, might fairly be induced to take for that of a foul Bone: Which I mentioned to the Doctor by the first return of the Post; and also, that I was farther encouraged in that Hope, by considering that the Blood, that was discharged at the first Opening, was not at all altered, neither was any Smell perceived, until after the lodging of those *Dossels*.

Whether the Doctor ever mentioned this my Opinion, to the *Surgeons* in Town, I know not; but when he returned to me, to have the Operation performed, he seemed discouraged by the Opinion the *Surgeons* gave of the Bones being foul. But I thought I might make bold to confirm him, in my former Opinion, the ill Smell ceasing without the Assistance of Medicines. The Consequence proved the Assertion: For when, by several Applications of the *Cauteries*, I had removed the whole Tumor, it was plain to me, the Bone was not affected; and the Part healed as smooth, and with as much Ease, and in as short a Time, as ever I met any thing of that Nature, and the Doctor continued well, without the least Disorder or Complaint, a Year and about Eight Months.

But then in *April* 1718. He shewed me a small *Ulcer*, near that Part of the Mouth that was before affected, and told me, He perceived it began upon eating some hot Meat, that stuck to it: At first this healed without much Trouble, but soon excoriated again; and then I could not again perfectly skin it: For as soon as it was almost healed, it would begin to excoriate a-fresh at the Edges, which is what is usual in *Phagedænical Ulcers*. And tho' I could digest it, and keep it easy, yet it got ground of me, and spread towards the Teeth; and, near the Root of One of the *Molares*, laid the Bone bare, which appeared to me at the first not to be injured, but being long exposed became foul. It not exfoliating in due Time, with the Tincture that is commonly used, I proposed the touching of it with a small *Cautery*, I being able very easily to come at it without making use of a *Cannula*; which, by confining the Heat, very much injures the neighbouring Parts: The good Effect of which Practice, of not making use of a *Cannula*, where you can conveniently omit it, I had good Experience of in Doctor *KEIL*'s former Case: For tho' he had several *Cannulas* made in *London*, by the best Hand, yet after Twice using of them, I told the Doctor, That if a Patient could be trusted, it would be much more easy to him, and the Surgeon would see much better to use the *Cautery*, than when obstructed by a *Cannula*. The Doctor was pleased with the Thought, and pressed me, at the next making use of the *Cautery*, to do it without the *Cannula*: The Advantage he had by it was, that it bore four Burnings, and said, It gave him not the Pain, or Trouble he had from but One before, and that the Parts were much less Disordered by it afterwards. But to return:

It will not I suppose be doubted, but that proper internal Means were all along made use of: But the *Ulcer* still appearing to me more threatening, his Friends pressed him, and I more than any, that he would go again to Town, and have the best Advice it could afford; and I resolved to accompany Him, in the Beginning of *August* 1718. And I cannot forbear saying I was surprized, when, upon a Consultation, my Brothers, *Palmer* and *Brown*, made light of it; and, without so much as hearing what I had to say, concluded, That it was chiefly owing to the Bones being foul; and that by drawing a Tooth or Two which they said were affected, and by Purging with *Mercurius dulcis*, all would be well; and so they took their Leave. Says the Doctor to me, "What say you to this?" I answered him, That I feared they would find themselves again mistaken as to the *Surgery* Part; and that as to the *Mercury*, though a good Medicine, He knew he had taken it already several Times, without any considerable Advantage. The Doctor smiled and said, "But since I came so far for Advice, I will not only give them a Tooth, but also try again what Effect *Mercury* may have."

Another Meeting was ordered, and the Tooth-Drawer to be there: Upon Drawing the Tooth, it appeared to be very sound. The First Dose he took of *Mercury*, whether by Cold, or any other Accident, I know not, very much disordered him. I could not conveniently be absent any longer, and therefore the next Day returned into the Country, and do not know how many more Doses the Doctor then took; but in a few Days I received a Letter from him, in which he said, "I know nothing that has succeeded right with me, since I came here: You know what State you left me in, and I was a great deal worse for some Days afterwards; though I hope the *Mercury* has had no ill Effect, yet I should have been loath to have been so swelled in those Parts, as I have been, willingly. The old *Ulcers* are not yet healed, they tell me indeed, there is no Appearance of any new Ones, and that the *most effectual* Methods, which have been taken here, will *infallibly* prevent every thing, &c."

But by his next, which I soon received, I had the melancholy News from him, That the *Ulcer* was broke out again larger than ever, and therefore that he would be down with me in a Day or two, and he came accordingly, but in a worse State than ever before. And though it again digested, and did as before near heal, yet the returns were quicker, and upon every new Eruption it was larger and worse; and so continued to be, notwithstanding all the good internal Methods continually used by the concurring Advice of Dr *Mead*, Dr *Friend*, and several other Eminent *Physicians*; which no doubt was owing to the malignant Nature of it.

And therefore in the Beginning of *February* last, I could no longer forbear expressing my Fears to the Doctor that it would terminate in a raging *Cancer*. He was too sensible of it, and told me, "That since I thought I could keep it within Bounds no longer, He was resolved to try what a *Salivation* would do:" And though I could say nothing as to the Advantage he might expect from it, yet I frankly owned to him, that if it was my own Case, I should be of his

Opinion, that I might make bolder with my self, than with any other Patient: But desired by all means, he would first hear if his Friends, the *Physicians* and *Surgeons* in *London*, had yet any other Method to propose, or else would approve of that. He wrote to them, the Answer was long in coming, which made the Doctor express himself to me with more Warmth, than I ever knew him to do before: (For he was a Man of the greatest Command of himself, as well as of the sweetest Temper) "What, says he, is not their Silence enough? And will not you, whom I take for my Friend (for fear of losing your Reputation) assist me in what I desire?" With a great deal more to assure me of his Confidence in me, and of his Opinion of my Ability to take Care of him in the Course. I am not so vain, as to mention all his kind Expressions, yet if it be desired, by any of his Friends, I will give them the Satisfaction of seeing the Letters I had from him, when he was absent from me in *London*.

At this Time his Brother, Doctor *John Keil*, came to him from *Oxford*; and, as I understood afterwards, had seen Dr *Friend* there, who was for having him salivated at *London*: But the Doctor being determined to the contrary, did not at that Time acquaint me with it, but began his Course, which I desired might be in the mildest Method, by small Doses of *Calomel*, encreased gradually, which Method pleased him very well: But Dr *Friend* (to whom Dr *John Keil* constantly sent an Account of our Proceedings) gave it as the Opinion of Mr *Palmer* and Mr *Brown*, that it should be done by *Unction*: I gave my Reason to the Patient against it, but they still pressed it, notwithstanding the ill Symptoms, that I thought, at that Time, forbad it; which Symptoms they had been acquainted with. They still persisting, I desired the Doctor would give me leave to write my Opinion my self to Mr *Brown*, which I did hastily in the following manner.

Good Brother,

I *Have seen Dr* Friend's *Letter to Dr* Keil; *and Dr* Friend *I understand has been so kind as to consult you, and several Others in the Case; whose Judgments, though I have all due Regard for, yet in the present Circumstances (though I give the Preference to* Unction *in some stubborn Cases) I dare not encourage it in this: For my Reason at first, for beginning so mildly, was, that in this uncommon Case, we might by degrees, make some Judgment of the Effects of* Mercury, *and then proceed accordingly: For had I not been prevented by the Accidents you have, by Dr* Friend, *been acquainted with, I should have been very desirous to have gone at least to the Heighth mentioned by Dr* Friend. *But since I find, by encreasing the Quantity of the Dose to a* Scruple *(of which he has taken four) it has not affected the Glands at all, or made him Spit the more; but his Stomach is much more oppressed by it, with vast Quantity of Phlegm, viscous to a degree I have not met with, and gives him more than common Disturbance, not to be relieved but by often Vomiting, to which purpose the* Turpith, *has answered very well for the present: My great Fear is, all things considered, that if I should proceed to* Unction, *and it should produce the same Effect, that it will be too many for him. If my Fears are too great, my more than common Concern and Friendship is some Excuse for me; as also I desire it may be to You, for this tedious Account from,* Sir,

Yours, &c.

Feb. 22d, 1718.

J . RU SH W O RT H.

I not receiving, in due Time, an Answer to this, and the Patient being reduced to a great Weakness, and to so great a Disorder, that he could not bear Talking to, I writ these few Lines for him to consider of.

Dear Sir,

*A*S *your Case now stands, I must own my self a Coward: Though Dr* Friend *is much mistaken to think I am either unacquainted with, or fear the common Accidents that often arise in Salivating: But that irregular and uncommon Effects are, in extraordinary Cases, produced by* Mercury, Hale's *Case is to me a sufficient Precedent, of which I have formerly told you the Particulars; and though your Friends in Town took no Notice of the unusual Disorder in your Stomach, yet I should think myself Inexcusable if I should not. And if, upon using an* Unction, *any irregular Ferments should again arise, weak as you now are, I should dread the Consequence. In these Circumstances, I think it most prudent for me, to advise you, to let what is already taken, go fairly off, and if you find it not effectual, you may with much better Prospect, when you have Strength, begin* de Nova, *by* Unction, *and have an Opportunity to have it done by the* infallible *Men.*

Upon this the Doctor no longer, at present, pressed me to use the *Unction*, and in a few Days, the Force of what he had taken being somewhat spent, he began to get Strength, and the very great Slough (which was one of the Accidents mentioned to Dr *Friend*) not only cast off, but also healed, as did also the old malignant *Ulcer*, and all the Parts of the Mouth looked very smooth and well; and the Doctor was very chearful, and in great Hopes of gaining the Point.

At this Time, it being eighteen Days since I wrote to Mr *Brown*, I received a Letter from him, in which he mentioned nothing to the Purpose. This, I must confess, did not a little warm me; and I the same Night wrote to him again, but never received any Answer: Perhaps he thought mine too hot; if so, if he desires it, both mine, and his that occasioned it, shall be produced.

The Doctor seeing what had been done to have so good Effect, and hoping what was before advised by Mr *Palmer* and Mr *Brown*, would effectually prevent any return of his Disorder, resolved to use a *Mercurial Unction*. He had now more Strength, and therefore I complied with him; I began with a small Quantity, and encreased it every Time, until I had used even a larger Quantity than had been proposed by Dr *Friend*: But it not in the least affected the Glands, or made him to spit near so much, as when he took the *Calomel*; neither did the *Unction* or *Calomel* produce the Smell, which generally attends *Mercurial* Courses; and to my great Surprize and Concern, whilst he was using the *Unction*, the *Ulcer* broke out again. And by this we were discouraged from proceeding any farther; and in due Time the Doctor endeavoured to Purge this off, but he had always so untoward a Constitution, that neither now, nor at any Time before, could he by Purges have any regular Evacuation; which was, no doubt in his Case, very Injurious to him.

Now I perfectly desponded: But a Friend and Kinsman of the Doctor's, a *Surgeon* of no small Reputation, assured him, that he had known, when other Methods failed, a *Mercurial Fumigation* had answered: And what is it that a rational Man will not try to prevent the excruciating Pains of a *Cancer?* When the Doctor mentioned this to me, I confessed I knew nothing of that Practice, and always had an ill Opinion of the Fumes of *Mercury*: And he also owned to me, that he was wholly unacquainted with it; but satisfied in his Friend, and therefore would try it: He began the Course according to his Friend's Directions; I never pretended to order any thing afterwards; but however still frequently visited my Good Friend, though with an aking Heart. The Fumigation not only made him spit, whilst he was using it, but also for some Hours afterwards; and the Patient continued to use it for several Days, but without any good Effect upon the *Ulcer*. In about ten Days after he had left off the Fumigation, a very hard Tumour began to arise, upon the Muscles of the lower Part of the Face and Neck, and increased very fast, and in a very short Time spread it self from Ear to Ear: and, by the Bulk, in a great measure prevented his Swallowing, and soon suffocated him. He was Chearful, and to all outward Appearance tolerably easy to the last, and had what he now desired, a gentle Release, *July 16, 1719*.

And thus, to the Misfortune of Mankind, it is manifest to me, that *Mercury* is not adequate to this *Herculean* Distemper: but however, this Case, and That I mentioned before to the Doctor, gives me good Reason to believe, that *Mercurials* do at least blunt the Acrimony of the Humour, and so procure Ease. For, though that Patient had most acute Pains, before he entered into a *Mercurial* Course, yet afterwards he was easy all a long, as he told me; for I was called in but a few Days before he died. These, and other melancholly Cases, should not however, I think, wholly discourage *Surgeons* from making rational Attempts upon a Distemper, which I fear is more frequently met with, than formerly, in this Part of the World: It is to be hoped, there is in Nature a Specific that may answer; and happy will that Man be who shall discover it. He will deserve to be placed next to the Great *Hippocrates*, and also to be rewarded, by the Publick, equally with him that shall find out the *Longitude*.

I will not pretend to determine, how far the Fumigation might contribute to the sudden growth of the Tumour mentioned, but I should be very glad that the *Surgeon* who recommended it, would be so ingenuous, as to vindicate himself, by giving Instances of it's Innocency, and of the Advantages he has met with in the Practice of it.

And now I heartily beg Pardon of the Friends of the Deceased, who shall give themselves the Trouble of Reading this Account, that I could not bring it into a narrower Compass.

Having truly related what was done, in the Case of Dr *Keil*, I hope it may appear, that I have acted an honest, and not an unskilful Part in it: If what was prescribed by others of greater Fame, when it came to be tried, had not better Success, I presume I shall no longer be blamed for it. No Man would willingly lose any Reputation, who is to live by it. I question not, but the best *Surgeons* in the World will allow, there are Cases for which there is no Remedy: And he who frankly owns thus much, no more loses any Reputation, than the Quack, that promises greater Matters than he afterwards performs, gets any: And I think they, who have censured me, would have done more ingenuously, if they would rather have looked upon the present Case as incurable by any *Surgeon*, than have thrown their Aspersions upon me, as not treating it properly.

N. B. The foregoing remarkable *Case* of Dr *Keil*, was published by Mr *Rushworth* of *Northampton*, Surgeon at *Oxford*, in the Year 17193. Under the *Imprimatur* of *Robert Shippen*, Vice-Can. *Oxon.*

Some curious Observations *made (by my Friend* John Ranby, *Esq*; *Surgeon to his Majesty's Household, and F. R. S.) in the* Dissection *of* Three Subjects, 1728.

T H E *first*, a Man aged 70 Years, who died of a Suppression of Urine, occasioned by a Stone stopping in the *Urethra*, just within the *Glans*, of the bigness of a Horse Bean. This Appearance, with the Symptoms that had attended this miserable Man, gave me reason to expect something remarkable in the urinary Passages. The *Ureters* and *Pelvis* were very much distended; which is common where great Numbers of Stones have descended down them, from the Kidneys to the Bladder. The Bladder contained about 60 Stones, the largest of which was about the Size of a Walnut, the others smaller; and just within the Neck, was a hard *Tumour*, as big as a Nutmeg, which almost closed the Orifice: and indeed the Situation of this Tumour was such, that it not only made the passing the *Catheter* very difficult, and hindered our feeling the Stones, by directing the Instrument upwards: but likewise would alone produce the Symptoms of the Stone in the Bladder, by obstructing the free Discharge of Urine through the *Urethra*, the inner Membrane of which appeared as if lacerated in several Places, and the Tube filled with a glutinous Matter tinged with Blood. On the back Part of the *Vesiculæ Seminales*, near the *Prostata*, were several *Stones*, as large as Peas, which closely adhered to the adjacent Membranes.

The *second*, a Boy aged 10 Years, killed by a Blow on the Skull; whose Spleen weighed two Pounds, and possessed almost all the left Side of the abdominal Cavity. The Bladder, when distended to its greatest Capacity, would not contain an *Ounce*.

The *third*, a Man aged 25, who died of a Pocky Hectick, and some Days before complained of a painful Swelling in the Testicle, which he said came the Night before. I examined it, and found it to be a *Hernia Aquosa*, and would have punctured it, if I had not felt (besides the Water) a hard Body, which I could by no Means reduce. In a few Days he died, which gave me an Opportunity of being satisfied. Opening the *Scrotum*, and separating the common Membranes to the *Processus Vaginalis*, it contained about 4 Ounces of Water, besides a great Part of the *Omentum*; some Portions of which adhered to the Bottom of the Cavity, and the *Albuginea* that immediately covers the Testicle.

It has been likewise thought proper to preserve a *small Treatise* of curing *Consumptions* by a new Method, of administring *Specific-Medicines*, more especially *such* as proceed from *Ulcers* of the *Lungs*.

This excellent Piece was written by the late eminent Mr *Thomas Nevett*, of *Fen-Church Street*, Surgeon.

A NEW

METHOD

Of Curing

CONSUMPTIONS

BY

Specific Medicines.

INTRODUCTION.

I Remember a remarkable Passage in some *Observations* upon the *Bermudus* Berries, by a Doctor of Physic in the Country, addressed to the Hon. *Robert Boyle*, Esq; who professeth he had been for 50 Years an exact Observer of the *Methodus Medendi*; yet saith the Doctor for my part I firmly believe, that (*Universal Evacuations* being premised) the greatest Cures wrought in the World, are by the use of *Specifical Medicines*. The higher the Attainments of any have been in Understanding, the more freely have they acknowledged that the greatest part of those *things* they *did know*, was the least of those *things* they *did not know*; such Men account it not shameful to renounce an Errour, tho' ever so ancient, when persuaded thereunto by Truth and plain Demonstration: There are other narrow Spirits (abundantly satisfied in their own Knowledge) who believe the *Art* of *Physic* hath been taught by our Ancestors, in such an absolutely perfect manner, as that nothing remains to the Industry and Diligence of Posterity; it being too much their Humour to undervalue every Medicine that they themselves are not Masters of, because they prefer their private Interest to the public Good: But in the mean time where is that cordial Love to Mankind, which is one of the Badges of true Christianity? Nay, where is the Exercise of Reason? For how can a Man give his Opinion against a thing that he never *heard of* before, or at least never *experienced*? I am sure, this unjustifiable Practice is the way to put a stop to all useful Knowledge and Improvements: It is therefore expected from the Ingenious and Candid Reader, that he should adhere to the Cause of Truth, by whomsoever it is pleaded, weigh every Invention, not in the deceitful *Balance* of *Custom*, but in the just and even *Scales* of *Reason*; approve what is agreeable, and reject what is contrary to it.

That I who am by Profession a Surgeon, should in such a polite and inquisitive Age, venture my Thoughts in public concerning a *Physical Case*, may be to some matter of Admiration, and to others of severe Censure; especially such as may think I have invaded their Province. As for the latter, I am persuaded nothing that I can say will remove their Prejudices; and for the former, I shall only tell them, that being alarmed by some of the *Symptoms* mentioned in the following Discourse, whereby I plainly perceived the Constitution of my own Body inclined to a *Consumptive State*, I strenuously applied my Mind to study the Nature of this *Disease*, and to find out, if possible, some noble Specific Medicines, which might indeed deserve that Name, and be able to oppose the growth of so fatal a Distemper, which hath insensibly flattered so many into the Chambers of Death. What I then laboured for, and searched after, I have since (by the Blessing of God) found, and with great Advantage experimented on my self and many others, and now think fit to disclose for the good of All, not doubting but if a more excellent Method and Medicine than hath hitherto been generally administered, or prescribed, be treasured up in the Hands of any Person whatsoever, he doth more faithfully perform the part of a just Steward, by a due Improvement, than a close Concealment of it. And on the same Account, I judge it more my Duty to serve my Native Country, than mind the Clamours of censorious Critics; not at all questioning but in a little time, the Efficacy of *these Medicines* will at once bring Health to the Patient, and Reputation to their Author: And the World will be convinced of the *Power* of these *Remedies*, by their Effects; tho' ignorant Persons may be apt to contemn and neglect, till their Opinions be altered by *Experience*, and their Prejudices removed by *Demonstration*.

Of the Nature, Causes, and Symptoms of Consumptions.

I. A *Consumption*, in general, is a wasting of all the solid parts of the Body, for want of a due Distribution, or Assimilation of the Nutritious Juices.

By some learned Men this is observed to be the *Endemical Distemper* of *England*; and indeed our *Weekly-Bills* at once declare both the Strength of the Disease, and the Weakness of the Medicines wherewith it's Cure hath been hitherto attempted. Besides, that which seems to justify this Observation, is the pernicious Custom of the Inhabitants of this island, who immoderately and unseasonably indulge their Appetites with several sorts of Meats and Drinks, whereby the Tone of the Stomach is so vitiated, as that it cannot perfectly ferment and volatilize the Chyle, which is commonly the internal procatartic Cause of most Distempers among us, and consequently of *Consumptions* from those Distempers, from whence comes a Colliquation of the Chyle in *Lienteries* and *Dysenteries*, tormenting *Cholic* and *Iliac* Pains, hypocondriac Melancholly, hysteric Fits, scorbutic Twitches, troublesome Catarrhs, sluggish Passage of the Chyle thro' the milky Veins, scrophulous Tumours and Inflammations of the mesenteric Glands, spasmodic Contractions or Convulsions of the Nerves, preternatural Fermentation of the Blood and Spirits, *Cachexies*, *Atrophies*, Obstructions, Fevers hectical, inflammatory and putrid, Exulcerations of the Lungs and *Marasmus*, with many other Diseases, whence come they originally and for the most part, but from the Weakness, ill Habit and Indisposition of the Stomach?

Now the proper Action of the Stomach is Chylification; for tho' the Meat we take into our Mouths receives some Alteration there in Mastication, by the fermenting Juice that flows from the salivatory Glands, together with the acrimonious Particles, and fermentaceous Spirits of Liquors which we drink, yet it is not turned into a thick white Juice, 'till it hath passed down thro' the *Oesophagus*, or Gullet, into the Stomach, where by the help of it's Fibres it is closely embraced, and mixed with specific fermentaceous Juices, separated by it's inner Coat, and impregnated by the Saliva, then by a convenient Heat there is made a mixture of all; for that the fermentaceous Particles entering into the Pores of the Meat, do pass thro' agitate and eliquate it's Particles, dissolving the whole *Compages*, in which the purer parts were intimately united with the Crass, and making them more fluid, so that they make another form of Mixture, and unite among themselves into the resemblance of a milky Cream, after which together with the thicker Mass with which they are yet involved, by the Constriction of the Stomach they pass down to the Guts, where by the Mixture of the Bile and Pancreatic Juice they are by another manner of Fermentation quite separated from the thicker Mass, and so are received by the Lacteal Vessels, as the thicker is ejected by Stool.

After the purer part of the Chyle hath been thus strained thro' the narrow and oblique Pores of the milky Veins, by the continual and peristaltic Motion of the Intestines, it is yet farther attenuated and diluted with a very thin and clear *Lympha* from the Glands of the Mesentery to expedite its passage thro' those numerous Meanders into the common Receptacle, from whence by the constant Supply of such like *Lympha* from the small Glands of the *Thorax*, it is safely conveyed thro' the *Ductus Chyliferus Thoracius*, subclavian Vein, and the *Vena Cava* into the Heart.

The Chyle now mingled with the Blood, passeth with it thro' the Arteries of the whole Body, and returns again with the Blood by the Veins to the Heart, undergoing many Circulations before it can be assimilated to the Blood; for every time the new infused Chyle passeth thro' the Heart with the Blood, the Particles of the one are more intimately mixed with those of the other, in it's Ventricles, and the Vital Spirit, and other active Principles of the Blood work upon the Chyle, which being full of Salt, Sulphur and Spirit, as soon as it's *Compages* is loosned by it's Fermentation with the Blood, the Principles having obtained the Liberty of Motion, do readily associate themselves, and are assimilated with such parts of the Blood as are of a like and suitable Nature.

After the Chyle hath been thus elaborated, it becomes fit as well to recruit the Mass of Blood, as to nourish the whole Body, seeing it consists of divers Principles and Parts of a different Nature; therefore, according to the various Use and Necessity of every part, and also that it may conform and fashion it self to the different Pores and Passages, it is severally appropriated; the most volatile and subtil part is separated in the Brain, and adapted to refresh the Animal Spirits, the glutinous to nourish the Body, and the sulphureous to revive the native Heat: And in it's Passage with the Blood thro' all the parts of the Body, all the Mass of Chyle that is capable of being turned into Blood is sanguified; the serous and saline part precipitated by the Kidneys, and evacuated by Sweats or insensible Transpirations, the bilious is deposited in the Liver, and the rest of its Excrements retire to the several Emunctories of the Body.

Thus it comes to pass by the wonderful Sagacity of Nature, such extraordinary Provision is made, that the purer part of the Chyle by these ways and means is more purified; and when it is thus purified and sublimed, it is more capable of reinforcing the Blood and Spirits, as also of corroborating the Tone of every particular Part: Whereas when the Chyle is sour and dispirited, the Blood necessarily becomes vappid, the animal Spirits which reside in the System of the Nerves are infected with a Morbid Disposition, and all parts of the Body begin to flag and waste. For indeed there is no other way to recruit the daily Expence of Blood and Spirits, but by a continual Influx of laudable Chyle into the Blood-Vessels, which Chyle is made by the Fermentative Juice of the Stomach, and this Fermentative Juice supplied from the Mass of Blood, so that there plainly appears to be a fixed Correspondence betwixt the Blood and the Chyle, and a necessary Dependance all the Humours in the Habit of the Body have on the Stomach; from whence it is reasonable to infer, That if the Chilifying Faculty of the Stomach be depraved, the Blood and Humours must necessarily sympathize therewith, and in a manner proportionable to the Distemper of this part.

II. The immediate Cause of a *Consumption* of the *Lungs* is store of sharp, malignant, waterish Humours, continually distilling upon the soft spungy Substance of the Lungs, stuffing, inflaming, impostumating, and exulcerating them, whereby their Action, which is Respiration, or a receiving-in and driving-out Air is depraved, as will more clearly appear by the following Description of these Parts. It will not be impertinent to our Discourse if we should usher in the Description of the *Lungs*, with a short Account of the *Trachea, Aspera Arteria,* or *Wind-pipe.*

III. The *Trachea* or *Aspera Arteria* is a long Pipe, consisting of Cartilages and Membranes, which beginning at the Throat or lower part of the Jaws, and lying upon the Gullet, descends into the *Lungs,* thro' which it spreads into many Branchings, and is commonly divided into two parts, the *Larynx* and *Bronchus*; the *Larynx* is the upper part of the Wind-pipe, the *Bronchus* is all the *Trachea* besides the *Larynx*, as well before as after it arrives at the *Lungs.*

The Substance of the *Lungs* is soft, spongy and rare, curiously compacted of most thin and fine Membranes, continued with the Ramifications of the *Trachea* or Wind-pipe, which Membranes compose an infinite number of little, round and hollow Vesicles, or Bladders, so placed as that there is an open Passage from the Branches of the *Aspera Arteria,* out of one into another, and all terminate at the outer Membrane that investeth the whole *Lungs*: These little Bladders by help of their muscular Fibres contract themselves in Expiration, and are dilated in Inspiration, partly by the Pressure of the Atmosphere, and partly by the elastic Power of the Air, insinuating it self into these Vesicles thro' the Windpipe and it's several Branches: Their Lobes are two, the right and left, parted by the *Mediastinum*, each of which is divided into many lesser Lobules, according to the Ramifications of the *Aspera Arteria*; they have all sorts of Vessels that are common to them with other parts, as Arteries, Veins, Nerves, Lympheducts, but peculiar to themselves they have their *Bronchia*, or the Branches of the Wind-pipe, for bringing-in and carrying-out Air so necessary to Life, that we cannot Live without it: And when we consider their admirable Structure, (as well as the Structure of every individual part of our Body) how ought we to adore the infinite Wisdom of our Creator! Now when these small Vesicles or Bladders are replete with extravasated *Serum*, or purulent Matter, the natural Tone of the *Lungs* is so weakned, that we cannot enjoy the Benefit of free and full Respiration, hard, scirrhous Tumours and Tubercles are bred, attended with a dry and troublesome Cough, Oppression of the Breast, difficult and short Breathing, preternatural Heats, Exulcerations, and other deplorable Symptoms, according to the Degrees of Obstruction, and different Nature of the included Humours.

IV. The external Procatartic Cause of a *Consumption* of the *Lungs* is cold Particles of Air, constipating the Pores of the Body, whereby the *Serum* which ought to expedite the Motion, and temperate the Heat of the Blood is separated from it, and thrown upon the Glands of the *Larynx*, and the spungy Substance of the Lungs themselves: For as the *Lympha* helps the Motion of the *Chyle*, so the *Serum* accelerates the Circulation of the Blood, being carried about with it thro' the smallest Capillary Vessels and remotest parts of the Body, lest it should be inflamed with a burning Heat, or stagnate by excessive Thickness; during which circular Motion they are both called by the same common Name, but when some Portion of *Serum* is separated from the Mass of Blood, and retreats to some one or more of the Emunctories; according to their various Dispositions, it derives a Name from those particular Parts on which it seizeth, as when it distils upon the Eyes, we call it *Opthalmia*, when upon the Nose *Coryza*, and when upon the *Thorax* it goes by the proper Name of a *Catarrh*.

Now forasmuch as there is nothing makes a Separation of the Blood more commonly than the want of usual Transpiration, so nothing more conduceth to the Preservation of Health, than that the Pores of the Body should continually let out the hot Streams and Vapours that arise from the Ebullition of the Blood; but when after taking Cold the Skin and Habit of the Body are on a sudden stopped up, that the sulphureous and waterish Excrements of the Blood cannot pass through the Pores, they are again resorbed into the Mass of Blood, from whence proceeds a feverish Disposition; unless they are carried off by Stool, or precipitated by the Kidneys, are sometimes translated to the Glandulous Parts of the *Lungs*, where by Degrees contracting more and more Heat and Sharpness they inflame and exulcerate these tender Parts.

Nevertheless tho' a *Consumption* of the *Lungs* is sometimes thus caused by taking Cold, yet this comes to pass but seldom, unless in such Bodies whose Mass of Blood being rendered Cachectic, thro' frequent Influxes of dispirited Chyle, is pre-disposed to receive, and unable to free it self from this New Influx of Catarrhous Rheum: For suppose Two Persons in like manner deprived of the Benefit of usual Transpiration, by some great Cold, which tho' troublesome in the beginning, because of a violent and continual Distillation of Extravasated *Serum* upon the Glandulous Coat of the Wind-pipe, and other adjacent Glands, yet in the One of these it survives not the accidental feverish Disposition of the Blood, occasioned by the Stoppage of the Pores: For as soon as the Ferment ceaseth, the separated Humours, partly for want of a new Influx of *Serum*, and partly by the natural Heat of these Parts, are concocted into a thick sort of Phlegm, and coughed up; after the Expectoration of which separated *Serum* the glandulous Parts presently recover their natural Tone, without any Remains of a Tumour, Cough, Shortness of Breath, or other Inconvenience; but in the other this feverish Ferment, occasioned by taking Cold, is not transitory, but so habitually fixed by means of some previous Indisposition, as to encrease the Effervescence and Colliquation of the Blood and Spirits; from whence all the Glands which are seated in the upper part of the *Larynx*, as also the glandulous Coat of the Wind-pipe it self are overflown with a Deluge of hot distempered Humours, the Substance of the *Lungs* distended with hard Tumours, the Branches of the Wind-pipe comprest, and the Wind-pipe it self from these Swellings irritated to Cough, by a continual tickling, which promotes a frequent spewing out of hot sharp Humours all along the *Aspera Arteria*, till at length these Tubercles growing very large, begin to inflame and suppurate; immediately upon the breaking or opening of those Apostemes, sometimes such a Flood of corrupted Matter is poured out of their Baggs or Cavities, into the Branches of the *Trachea*, as compleatly suffocates and choaks the Patient; but at other times this Purulent Matter, mixt with streaks of Blood, and some thin Phlegm that is continually discharged from the glandulous Coat of the Wind-pipe, is coughed up by degrees, and then this deplorable Case requires Specific Medicines, to cleanse and heal these Ulcers.

V. Such kind of *Consumptions* whose Original is store of malignant acrimonious Humours, which are most apt to inflame and putrify, may be termed acute, when compared to others that proceed from Humours more mild and benign. There may be likewise some difference made by omitting Bleeding, and committing some egregious Errors in Diet, Exercise, Passions of the Mind, or any other of the *Non-Naturals*: However, all *Consumptions* of the *Lungs* ought to be reckoned in the Number of Chronical Distempers, because they are contracted and augmented by degrees, and no other way to be remedied; yet this doth not prove them incurable in their own Nature, for Reason and Experience both teach the contrary: And indeed I must confess, it was from the marvelous Success of these Remedies that I first imbibed this Notion, *viz. Ulcers* of the *Lungs* are in themselves curable. Sometimes a Fever or other acute Distemper may be jugulated, when either Nature or Art carries off the Morbific Matter by a sudden *Crisis* or plentiful Evacuation, but all hopes of dispatching a confirmed *Consumption* of the *Lungs* instantly are groundless, seeing many inveterate Obstructions must be removed, abundance of tough glutinous Humours attenuated and evacuated, the whole Mass of Blood and Spirits rectified, the Habit of the Body meliorated, and the Tone of several parts recovered, before we can eradicate this fixed Distemper.

What will be the Issue and Result of this *Consumptive-Disease*, may rationally be prognosticated from it's several Stages or Degrees: For when the Mass of Blood by a continual Influx of sour dispirited Chyle is reduced to a sharp and hectical State, and the *Serum* which is separated from this corrupted Blood only stuffs the Bladders and Glandules which are dispersed thro' the Body of the Lungs, this Distemper may be said to be in it's Infancy or beginning, (and if sovereign Remedies were then presented, they might obtain an easy Conquest) but the Increase is attended with a greater Distention of the Glands and Bladders, as also an Inflammation of these Tubercles tending to suppuration: For when the Animal Spirits which are necessary to the natural Fermentation of the Blood are vitiated with unwholesome Particles of a foggy and thick Air, and the Humour which for a long time hath been contained in the Baggs or Cavities of the Lungs is over-heated by some extraordinary Ebullition or Fermentation of the Blood, with a total Suppression of Expectoration, the Cough becomes more violent, the Fever inflammatory, and all parts more tabid. In it's further Progress or State all Symptoms advance apace towards their Extremity, Suppuration now succeeds the Inflammation of these Tubercles, for that the Purulent Matter is either breeding or already made, the Inflammatory Hectic is changed into a putrid Intermitting Fever, attended with an Universal Colliquation of the Nutritious Juices and plentiful Separation of them from the Mass of Blood by all ways of Evacuation that Nature affords; whence the Patients strength suddainly decays, and in a short time he is reduced to the highest State of a *Marasmus*, with an *Hippocratic* Face.

VI. Thus having demonstrated to the meanest Capacity the Power of this prevailing Evil, with it's efficient and material Causes, Reason it self presently suggests nothing less than great and noble Medicines can tame a Distemper so formidable. It is no less obvious to the Understanding of every one that professeth any thing of Physic, that the sooner the Cure is begun the better, the more moderate the Patient is in the use of the Six *Non-Naturals*, the more likely to succeed; the Spring-time is the best Season, Universals are to be premised, extraordinary Symptoms and Circumstances peculiarly attended, and such like things must run through the whole Course of Practice.

No doubt but the Chalibeate Mineral Waters when impregnated with the Volatile Salts and Spirits of a serene Air, pleasant Society, delightful Recreations, Morning and Evening Walks, regular Diet, Freedom from Business, vexatious Thoughts, Exercise4, and the rest may be serviceable: But if the *Jesuit* were sentenced to perpetual Exile, I think the Consumptive have no reason excessively to lament, for I can tell them who hath a Febrifuge Antihectical, without a Grain of the *Jesuit*, more excellent far than the *Peruvian* Bark, because it makes a safe, not a treacherous Peace, and can give a Reason of it's working so stupendiously, tho' they who know not how a thing can be done, think it impossible to be done.

For my part, I do not believe any Medicine can work a Cure in the way of a Charm, yet they who either know or use no other (at least for the most part) than ordinary Medicines, cannot conceive how such wonderful Effects can be wrought, unless by Inchantment5.

The common Method of Cure is by Bleeding to abate the Effervescence or Colliquation of the Blood, and prevent the Tumour and Inflammation of the Lungs, by Vomits to relieve the Stomach opprest with store of ill Humours, and remove divers Obstructions of several Bowels and small Vessels, by Stomach-Purges gently to carry down the peccant Humours; and lastly by Diuretics and Diaphoretics with some mixture of an Opiate, plentifully to carry off the Colliquated *Serum* by Urine, or the Pores of the Skin, without raising a fresh Catarrh by a new Commotion of the Blood. After a due Administration of these universal Evacuations, (which in their respective Seasons are highly necessary) the frequent Use of Pectoral Apozems and Pulmonary Linctuses is next enjoined, to retund the Acrimony of the Humours which ouze out of the Wind-pipe, by their mucilaginous and incrassating Quality, and so mitigate the troublesome Cough. How far serviceable to this end and purpose the neatest Forms of such Dispensations that I ever yet saw may be, I will not dispute, only this I must take leave to say, because to me (as also to the unprejudiced I humbly conceive) it seems evident that such fulsom Ingredients of which they are compounded, are more apt to spoil a weak than recover a lost Stomach, and consequently not the fittest Medicines Consumptive Persons may have recourse to: For how many by woful Experience have found the constant and frequent use of such Anti-Stomachics led them from one Degree of this Malady to another, 'till their decaying Appetite hath been quite overthrown, (and consequently their hectic Heat inflamed) their Bodies so emaciated, as to render them uncapable of necessary Evacuations, and they themselves at last given over to a Milk Diet, Asses Milk, some Chalibeate Mineral Waters, or such like Liquids, to which the poor distressed Stomach ecchoes aloud, *Miserable Comforters all!* If therefore I can, as I have Reason to believe, with Medicines less offensive in Quantity, and more useful in Quality, restore the lost Appetite, and do the same, if not greater Service towards the Concocting and Expectorating that load of separated *Serum* with which the Pipes of the Lungs are stuffed, (which will easily be perceived by the Patient in a few Weeks with due Care and Management) I think I have gained a great Point, forasmuch as the Recovery of the Stomach may reasonably be looked upon as an Earnest of the Cure.

The Medicines I do here recommend to my Countrymen as Specific in the Cure of *Consumption* of the *Lungs*, arising from the fore-mentioned Causes, have a peculiar Faculty of warming, comforting and strengthening weak

Stomachs, attenuating and gently carrying off that load of Tartareous Matter which is lodged in their rugous Coat, depraving both Appetite and Digestion. In their Passage thro' the whole Circumference of the Guts, they likewise dissolve that crusted Slime and Filth which hinders the Pressure of the Chyle into the Milky Vessels by the Peristaltic Motion of their Spiral Fibres: Thus having removed these Fundamental Obstructions, they hasten together with the Chylous Mixture, which by this time is somewhat Invigorated towards the Relief of the Sanguineous Mass, presently upon their Conjunction the Blood revives, and by degrees becomes brisk and vigorous, able to cope with, and give some check to the preternatural hectic Heat, stop the Influx of the Rheum into the Glandulous Substance of the Lungs, concoct that which is already collected, and release the Animal Spirits, intangled with a vitious disposition of the Nervous Juice. Having gained these Advantages, things begin to look with another manner of Aspect, the Habit of the Body grows firmer, the Mind chearfuller, the Countenance fresh and brisk, the emaciated Parts gather Flesh and Strength, the Lungs and Glands of the *Larynx* recover their natural Tone, and the whole Constitution improves towards a State of Health. Moreover, These *Anti-Phthisics* are really impregnated with such Volatile Spirits and Salts, that as Lightning they penetrate the remotest Corners of the Body, exterminating the very Seeds and Roots of this grievous Disease, powerfully and effectually, yet pleasantly and securely, if plentifully taken in the manner of a Diet: For thus in time they chear up the drooping Animal Spirits, fortify the System of the Nerves, and so influence the whole Sanguineous Mass, as that the Blood it self becomes the most precious of all natural Balsoms, marvellously cleansing the putrid *Ulcers* of the *Lungs*, and finally reducing them to a perfect *Cicatrix*.

Wherefore let none be deceived by the flattering Nature of this Distemper in the beginning, nor give themselves over for lost in the highest State, because these reviving Cordials are calculated for the weakest Constitutions, seeing at the same time they offend the Diseased Matter on the one Hand, they support Nature from sinking under any Evacuations on the other. It is therefore my Advice to the *Consumptive*, or *Consumptively-inclined*, and their Interest (by way of Prevention) to acquaint themselves in time with these Sovereign Antidotes. Better Counsel I cannot give to the best of my Friends, if they are desirous to save themselves a great deal of Pain and Misery, as well as Charges, and render their Lives comfortable to themselves and serviceable to others.

The Warmness of these Medicines, which is the only Objection that ever I met with in the use of them, is so far from being a real Discouragement, as that upon serious and judicious Considerations, it becomes a Notable Argument to enforce the taking of them; for otherwise they would be too weak to engage the Original Cause of hectic, burning and putrid Fevers; whereas by this active Principle of Heat, they work so effectually upon the whole Mass of Chyle, as to separate the sharp and dispirited from the nutritious Particles thereof, thoroughly insinuate themselves into all the Avenues of the Adversary, cut and divide the tough viscous Humours which distemper the Veins, Arteries and Nerves, destroy the Acidity of the Nervous Juice, recover the Natural Temper of the Animal Spirits, sweeten the Mass of Blood, by separating the Impurities thereof by the Cutaneous Glands, gently forcing a Transpiration of the Feverish Particles of the whole, and so banish that Preternatural Heat which is Proof to all common Remedies. And that Diseases which carry in their outward Appearance a shew of preternatural Heat are thus to be treated with warm Medicines, is indeed observable to every discerning Eye: For the most malignant Fevers are attacked and conquered by the briskest and warmest *Alexipharmics* and the most violent *Erysipelas*, or St *Anthony's Fire*, is discussed and breathed out by strong and spirituous Fomentations, but are both of them exasperated by refrigerating or cooling Medicines, and their preternatural Heat more and more increased, till the one at length terminates in the *cold sweats of Death*, and the other in a compleat *Mortification*.

To multiply Encomiums of this kind is remote from my intended Brevity, therefore take this remarkable one for all: The Efficacy of *Specific Medicines* may be experienced from Mr *Boyle*'s unparalelled Treatise, herein referred to, and from the full Descriptions I have given any Chymist of Eminence, upon consulting each respective Patient's Case, can effectually prepare them. But I would more particularly recommend for this Purpose the Skilful Mr *Boyle Godfrey*, in *Covent-Garden*.

THO. NEVETT.

A

MODEST DEFENSE

OF

PUBLICK STEWS

Price 2*s.* 6*d.*

THE NATURAL

SECRET HISTORY

OF

BOTH SEXES:

OR,

A Modest Defense

OF

PUBLIC STEWS.

With an Account of the Present State
of WHORING in these Kingdoms.

By *LUKE OGLE*, Esq;

THE FOURTH EDITION.

LONDON:

Printed in the YEAR M.DCC.XL.

TO THE

SOCIETIES

FOR

Reformation of Manners.

GENTLEMEN,

THE great Pains and Diligence You have employ'd in the Defence of Modesty and Virtue, give You an undisputed Title to the Address of this Treatise; tho' it is with the utmost Concern that I find myself under a Necessity of writing it, and that after so much Reforming, there should be any Thing left to say upon the Subject, besides congratulating You upon Your happy Success. It is no small Addition to my Grief to observe, that Your Endeavours to suppress Lewdness have only serv'd to promote it; and that this *Branch* of *Immorality* has *grown* under Your Hands, as if it was *prun'd* instead of being *lopp'd*. But however Your ill Success may grieve, it cannot astonish me: What else could we hope for, from Your persecuting of poor strolling Damsels? From your stopping up those *Drains* and *Sluices* we had to let out Lewdness? From your demolishing those *Horn-works* and *Breast-works* of Modesty? Those *Ramparts* and *Ditches* within which the Virtue of our Wives and Daughters lay so conveniently *intrench'd?* An Intrenchment so much the safer, by how much the Ditches were harder to be fill'd up. Or what better could we expect from Your Carting of Bawds, than that the Great Leviathan of Leachery, for Want of these Tubs to play with, should, with one Whisk of his Tail, overset the *Vessel* of Modesty? Which, in her best Trim, we know to be somewhat *leaky*, and to have a very unsteady *Helm*.

An ancient Philosopher compares Lewdness to a wild, fiery, and headstrong young Colt, which can never be broke till he is rid into a Bog: And *Plato*, on the same Subject, has these Words; *The Gods*, says he, *have given us one disobedient and unruly Member, which, like a greedy and ravenous Animal that wants Food, grows wild and furious, till having imbib'd the Fruit of the common Thirst, he has plentifully besprinkled and bedewed the Bottom of the Womb.*

And now I have mentioned the Philosophers, I must beg Your Patience for a Moment, to hear a short Account of their Amours: For nothing will convince us of the irresistible Force of Love, and the Folly of hoping to suppress it, sooner than reflecting, that those venerable *Sages*, those Standards of Morality, those great *Reformers* of the World, were so sensibly touch'd with this tender Passion.

Socrates confess'd, that, in his old Age, he felt a strange tickling all over him for five Days, only by a Girl's touching his Shoulder.

Xenophon made open Profession of his passionate Love to *Clineas*.

Aristippus of *Cyrene*, writ a lewd Book of ancient Delights; he compar'd a Woman to a House or a Ship, that was the better for being used: He asserted, that there was no Crime in Pleasure, but only in being a Slave to it: And often used to say, I *enjoy* Lais, *but* Lais *does not enjoy me*.

Theodorus openly maintain'd, that a wise Man might without Shame or Scandal, keep Company with common Harlots.

Plato, our great Pattern for chaste-Love, proposes, as the greatest Reward for public Service, that he who has perform'd a signal Exploit, should not be deny'd any amorous Favour. He writ a Description of the Loves of his Time, and several amorous Sonnets upon his own Minions: His chief Favorites were *Asterus, Dio, Phædrus*, and *Agatho*; but he had, for Variety, his Female Darling *Archeanassa*; and was so noted for Wantonness, that *Antisthenes*, gave him the Nick-name of *Satho*, i. e. *Well-furnish'd.*

Polemo was prosecuted by his Wife for Male-Venery.

Crantor made no Secret of his Love to his Pupil *Arcesilaus*.

Arcesilaus made Love to *Demetrius* and *Leocharus*; the last, he said, he would fain have open'd: Besides, he publickly visited the two *Elean* Courtezans, *Theodota* and *Philæta*, and was himself enjoy'd by *Demochares* and *Pythocles*: He suffer'd the last, he said, for Patience-sake.

Bion was noted for debauching his own Scholars.

Aristotle, the first *Peripatetic*, had a Son call'd *Nichomacus*, by his

Concubine *Herpilis*: He lov'd her so well, that he left her in his Will a Talent of Silver, and the Choice of his Country-Houses; that, as he says, the Damsel might have no Reason to complain: He enjoy'd, besides the Eunuch *Hermias*, others say only his Concubine *Pythais*, upon whom he writ a Hymn, call'd, *The Inside.*

Demetrius Phalereus, who had 360 Statues in *Athens*, kept *Lamia* for his Concubine, and at the same time was himself enjoy'd by *Cleo*: He writ a Treatise, call'd, *The Lover*, and was nick-nam'd by the Courtezans, *Charito*, *Blespharus*, i. e. *A Charmer of Ladies*; and *Lampetes*, i. e. *A great Boaster of his Abilities.*

Diogenes, the *Cynic*, us'd to say, that Women ought to be in common, and that Marriage was nothing but a Man's getting a Woman in the Mind to be lain with: He often us'd Manual Venery in the public Market-place, with this Saying. *Oh! that I could assuage my Hunger thus with rubbing of my Stomach!*

But what Wonder if the old *Academics*, the *Cyrenaics*, and *Peripatetics*, were so lewdly wanton, when the very *Stoics*, who prided themselves in the Conquest of all their other Passions, were forc'd to submit to this?

Zeno, indeed, the Founder of that Sect, was remarkable for his Modesty, because he rarely made Use of Boys, and took but once an ordinary Maid-Servant to Bed, that he might not be thought to hate the Sex; yet, in his *Commonwealth*, he was for a Community of Women; and writ a Treatise, wherein he regulated the Motions of getting a Maidenhead, and philosophically prov'd Action and Reaction to be equal.

Chrysippus and *Apollodorus* agree with *Zeno* in a Community of Women, and say, that a wise Man may be in Love with handsome Boys.

Erillus, a Scholar of *Zeno*'s, was a notorious Debauchee.

I need not mention the *Epicureans* who were remarkable for their Obscenity.

Epicurus used to make a Pander of his own Brother; and his Scholar, the Great *Metrodorus*, visited all the noted Courtezans in *Athens*, and publicly kept the famous *Leontium*, his Master's *Quondam* Mistress. Yet, if you will believe *Laertius*, he was every Way a good Man.

But what shall we say of our Favourite *Seneca*, who, with all his *Morals*, could never acquire the Reputation of *Chastity*? He was indeed somewhat Nice in his Amours, like the Famous *Flora*, who was never enjoy'd by any Thing less than a Dictator or a Consul; for he scorn'd to intrigue with any Thing less than the Empress.

Now, if those Reverend School-Masters of Antiquity, were so loose in their Seminals, shall we, of this Age, set up for Chastity? Have our *Oxford Students* more Command of their Passions than the *Stoics*? Are our Young *Templars* less Amorous than *Plato*? Or, is an *Officer* of the Army less Ticklish in the Shoulder than *Socrates*?

But I need not waste any Rhetoric upon so evident a Truth; for plain and clear Propositions, like Windows painted, are only the more Obscure the more they are adorn'd.

I will now suppose, that you have given up the Men as Incorrigible; since You are convinc'd, by Experience, that even Matrimony is not able to reclaim them. Marriage, indeed, is just such a Cure for Lewdness, as a Surfeit is for Gluttony; it gives a Man's Fancy a Distaste to the particular Dish, but leaves his Palate as Luxurious as ever: for this Reason we find so many marry'd Men, that, like *Sampson*'s Foxes, only do more Mischief for having their Tails ty'd. But the Women, You say, are weaker Vessels, and You are resolv'd to make them submit; rightly judging, if You cou'd make all the Females Modest, it would put a considerable Stop to Fornication. It is great Pity, no doubt, so Fine a Project should Miscarry: And I would willingly entertain Hopes of seeing one of these *Bridewell* Converts. In the mean Time it would not be amiss, if You chang'd somewhat your present Method of Conversion, especially in the Article of Whipping. It is very possible, indeed, that leaving a Poor Girl Penny-less, may put her in a Way of living Honestly, tho' the want of Money was the only Reason of her living otherwise; and the stripping of her Naked, may, for aught I know, contribute to Her Modesty, and put Her in a State of Innocence; but surely, *Gentlemen*, You must all know, that Flogging has a quite contrary Effect. This Project of pulling down Bawdy-houses to prevent Uncleanness, puts me in Mind of a certain Over-nice Gentleman, who cou'd never fancy his Garden look'd sweet, till he had demolish'd a Bog-house that offended his Eye in one Corner of it; but it was not long before every Nose in the Family was convinc'd of His Mistake. If Reason fails to Convince, let us profit by Example: Observe the Policy of a Modern Butcher, persecuted with a Swarm of Carnivorous Flies; when all his Engines and Flyflaps have prov'd ineffectual to defend his Stall against the Greedy Assiduity of those Carnal Insects, he very Judiciously cuts off a Fragment, already blown, which serves to hang up for a Cure; and thus, by sacrifising a Small Part, already Tainted, and not worth Keeping, he wisely secures the Safety of the Rest. Or, let us go higher for Instruction, and take Example by the Grazier, who far from denying his Herd the Accustom'd Privilege of Rubbing, when their Sides are Stimulated with sharp Humours, very Industriously fixes a Stake in the Center of the Field, not so much, you may imagine, to Regale the Salacious Hides of his Cattle, as to preserve his Young Trees from Suffering by the Violence of their Friction.

I could give You more Examples of this Kind, equally full of Instruction, but that I'm loth to detain You from the Perusal of the following Treatise; and at the same Time Impatient to have the Honour of Subscribing Myself

Your Fellow-Reformer,

and Devoted Servant,

PHIL - PORNEY.

PREFACE.

LEST any inquisitive Reader should puzzle his Brains to find out why this *Foundling* is thus clandestinely dropt at his Door, let it suffice him, that the *Midwife* of a Printer was unwilling to help bring it into the World, but upon that Condition, or a much harder, that of my openly *Fathering* it. I could make many other reasonable Apologies, if requisite: For, besides my having follow'd the modest Example of several other pious *Authors*, such as that of Εικων Βασιλικη, of the *Whole Duty of Man*, &c. who have studied rather their Country's Publick Good, than their own Private Fame; I think, I have also play'd the Politick Part: for should my *Off-spring* be defective, why let it fall upon the Parish. On the other hand, if accidentally it prove hopeful, 'tis certain I need be at no further Trouble. There will then be *Parents* enough ready to own the *Babe*, and take it upon themselves. Adoption amongst the *Machiavellian* Laws of the *Muses* is strictly kept up, and every day put in Practice: How few of our now bright *Noblemen* would otherwise have *Wit*? How many of our present thriving *Poets* would else want a *Dinner*? 'Tis a vulgar Error to imagine Men live upon their own Wits, when generally it is upon others Follies; a Fund that carries by much the best Interest, and is by far upon the most certain Security of any: The *Exchequer* has been shut up, the *Bank* has stopt Payment, *South-Sea* has been demolish'd, but *White's* was never known to fail; and indeed how should it, when almost every Wind blows to *Dover*, or *Holyhead*, some fresh *Proprietor* amply qualified with sufficient *Stock*.

I am in some pain for the Event of this *Scheme*, hoping the *Wicked* will find it too Grave, and fearing the *Godly* will scarce venture beyond the Title-Page: And should they, *even*, I know they'll object, 'tis here and there interwoven with too ludicrous Expressions, not considering that a dry Argument has occasion for the larding of Gaiety to make it the better relish and go down. Besides, finding by the exact Account tack'd to that most edifying *Anti-Heidegger* Discourse,6 that eighty six Thousand Offenders have been lately punish'd, and that four hundred Thousand religious Books have been distributed about *Gratis* (not to mention the numberless Three-penny Jobs daily publish'd to no Ends, or Purpose, but the *Author*'s;) I say, finding all these Measures have been taken, and that Lewdness still so much prevails, I thought it highly proper to try this Experiment, being fully convinc'd that opposite Methods often take place. Own, *Preferment-Hunter!* when sailing on with the Tide avails nothing, does not tacking about steer you sometimes into that snug Harbour, an Employment? Speak *Hibernian Stallion!* when a meek fawning Adoration turns to no Account, does not a pert assuming Arrogance frequently forward, nay, gain the critical Minute? And say,7 *Mesobin!* where a Purge fails, is not a Vomit an infallible *Recipe* for a Looseness?

To conclude; when my Arguments are impartially examin'd, I doubt not but my Readers will join with me, that as long as it is the Nature of Man (and *Naturam expellas furca licet usque recurret*) to have a Salt *Itch* in the Breeches, the *Brimstone* under the Petticoat will be a necessary Remedy to *lay* it; and let him be ever so sly in the Application, it will still be found out: What avails it then to affect to conceal that which cannot be concealed, and that which if carried on openly and above-board, would become only less detrimental, and of consequence more justifiable?

Be the Success of this Treatise as it happens, the Good of Mankind is my only Aim; nor am I less hearty or zealous in the Publick Welfare of my Country, than that Noble Pattern of Sincerity, Bishop *B——t*, who finishes his Preface with the following Paragraph. *And now, O my G—, the G— of my Life, and of all my Mercies, I offer this Work to Thee, to whose Honour it is chiefly intended; that thereby I may awaken the World to just Reflections on their own Errors and Follies, and call on them to acknowledge thy Providence, to adore it, and ever to depend on it.*

A

Modest Defence, &c.

T H E R E is nothing more idle, or shows a greater Affectation of Wit, than the modern Custom of treating the most grave Subjects with Burlesque and Ridicule. The present Subject of *Whoring*, was I dispos'd, would furnish me sufficiently in this kind, and might possibly, if so handled, excite Mirth in those who are only capable of such low Impressions. But, as the chief Design of this Treatise is to promote the general Welfare and Happiness of Mankind, I hope to be excus'd, if I make no farther Attempts to please, than are consistent with that Design. The Practice of *Whoring* has, of late Years, become so universal, and its Effects so prejudicial to Mankind, that several Attempts have been made to put a Stop to it; and a certain *Society* of Worthy *Gentlemen* have undertaken that Affair with a Zeal truly commendable, tho' the Success does but too plainly make it appear, that they were mistaken in their Measures, and had not rightly consider'd the Nature of this Evil, which we are all equally sollicitous to prevent, however we may differ in our Opinions as to the Manner. And tho' the Method I intend to propose, of erecting *Publick Stews* for that purpose, may seem at first sight somewhat ludicrous, I shall, nevertheless, make it appear to be the only Means we have now left for redressing this Grievance. As this Redress is the whole Scope and Design of this Treatise, I hope to be acquitted of my Design, when I have prov'd the following Propositions: That *publick Whoring* is neither so criminal in itself, nor so detrimental to the *Society*, as *private Whoring*; and that the encouraging of *publick Whoring*, by erecting *Stews*, will not only prevent most of the ill Consequences of this Vice, but even lessen the *Practice* of *Whoring* in general, and reduce it to the narrowest Bounds which it can possibly be contain'd in. But before we proceed, it is requisite that we examine what those mischievous Effects are which *Whoring* naturally produces, that we may the better judge whether or no they will be prevented by this Scheme.

The greatest Evil that attends this Vice, or could well befall Mankind, is the

Propagation of that infectious Disease, called the *French-Pox*, which in two Centuries, has made such incredible Havock all over *Europe*. In these Kingdoms it so seldom fails to attend *Whoring*, now-a-days mistaken for *Gallantry* and *Politeness*, that a hale, robust Constitution is esteem'd a Mark of Ungentility; and a healthy young Fellow is look'd upon with the same View, as if he had spent his Life in a Cottage. Our Gentlemen of the Army, whose unsettled way of Life makes it inconvenient for them to marry, are hereby very much weaken'd and enervated, and render'd unfit to undergo such Hardships as are necessary for defending and supporting the Honour of their Country: And our Gentry in general seem to distinguish themselves by an ill State of Health, in all probability the Effect of this pernicious Distemper: for the Secrecy which most People are obliged to in this Disease, makes the Cure of it often ineffectual; and tho' the Infection itself may possibly be remov'd, yet for want of taking proper Methods, it generally leaves such an ill Habit of Body as is not easily recover'd. 'Tis to this we seem to owe the Rise of that Distemper, the *King's-Evil*, never known till the *French Disease* began to prevail here. But what makes this Mischief the more intolerable, is, that the Innocent must suffer by it as well as the Guilty; Men give it to their Wives, Women to their Husbands, or perhaps their Children; they to their Nurses, and the Nurses again to other Children; so that no Age, Sex, or Condition can be intirely safe from the Infection.

Another ill Effect of this Vice, is, its making People profuse, and tempting them to live beyond what their Circumstances will admit of; for if once Men suffer their Minds to be led astray by this unruly Passion, no worldly Consideration whatever will be able to stop it; and Wenching as it is very expensive in itself, without the ordinary Charges of Physic or Children, often leads Men into a thousand other Vices to support its Extravagance: Besides, after the Mind has once got this extravagant Turn, there naturally follows a Neglect and Contempt of Business; and Whoring of itself disposes the Mind to such a sort of Indolence, as is quite inconsistent with Industry, the main Support of any, especially a trading, Nation.

The murdering of Bastard Infants is another Consequence of this Vice, by much worse than the Vice itself: and tho' the Law is justly severe in this Particular, as rightly judging that a Mind capable of divesting itself so intirely of Humanity, is not fit to live in a civiliz'd Nation: yet there are so many ways of evading it, either by destroying the Infants before their Birth, or suffering them afterwards to die by wilful Neglect, that there appears but little Hope of putting any Stop to this Practice, which, besides the Barbarity of it, tends very much to dispeople the Country. And since the Prosperity of any Country is allow'd to depend, in a great measure, on the Number of its Inhabitants, the *Government* ought, if it were possible, to prevent any Whoring at all, as it evidently hinders the Propagation of the Species: How many thousand young Men in this Nation would turn their Thoughts towards Matrimony, if they were not constantly destroying that Passion, which is the only Foundation of it? And tho' most of them, sooner or later, find the Inconvenience of this irregular Life, and think fit to confine themselves to One, yet their Bodies are so much enervated, by the untimely or immoderate Increase of this Passion, together with the Relics of Venereal Cures, that they beget a most wretched, feeble, and sickly Offspring: We can attribute it to nothing else but this, that so many of our ancient Families of Nobles are of late extinct.

There is one thing more we ought to consider in this Vice, and that is the Injury it does to particular Persons and Families; either by alienating the Affections of Wives from their Husbands, which often proves prejudicial to both, and sometimes fatal to whole Families; or else by debauching the Minds of young Women, to their utter Ruin and Destruction: for the Reproach they must undergo, when a Slip of this nature is discover'd, prevents their marrying in any Degree suitable to their Fortune, and by degrees hardens them to all Sense of Shame; and when they have once overcome that, the present View of Interest as well as Pleasure, sways them to continue in the same Course, till at length they become common Prostitutes.

These are the several bad Effects of Whoring; and it is an unhappy Thing, that a Practice so universal as this is, and always will be, should be attended with such mischievous Consequences: But since few or none of them are the necessary Effects of Whoring, consider'd in itself, but only proceed from the Abuse and ill Management of it; our Business is certainly to regulate this Affair in such sort as may best prevent these Mischiefs. And I must here beg pardon of those worthy *Gentlemen* of the *Society*, if I can't conceive how the Discouragement they have given, or rather attempted to give, to publick Whoring, could possibly have the desired Effect. If this was a Vice acquired by Habit or Custom, or depended upon Education, as most other Vices, there might be some Hopes of suppressing it; and then it would, no doubt, be commendable to attack it, without Distinction, in whatever Form or Disguise it should appear: But alas! this violent Love for Women is born and bred with us; nay, it is absolutely necessary to our being born at all: And however some People may pretend, that unlawful Enjoyment is contrary to the Law of *Nature*, this is certain, that Nature never fails to furnish us largely with this Passion, tho' she is often sparing to bestow upon us such a Portion of Reason and Reflection as is necessary to curb it.

That long Course of Experience which most of these *Gentlemen* have had in the World, and which is of so great Use in other Cases, may probably occasion their Mistake in this; for Age is very liable to forget the violence of youthful Passions, and, consequently, apt to think them easier curb'd: whereas if we consider the true Source of Whoring, and the strong Impulse of Nature that way, we shall find, it is a Thing not to be too violently restrain'd; lest, like a Stream diverted out of its proper Channel, it should break in and overflow the neighbouring *Inclosures*.

History affords us several Instances of this Truth; I shall mention but one, and that is of Pope *Sixtus* the Fifth, who was so strictly severe in the Execution of Justice, if such Severity may be call'd Justice, and particularly, against Offenders of this kind, that he condemned a young Man to the Galleys, only for snatching a Kiss of a Damsel in the Street: yet notwithstanding this his *Holiness*'s Zeal, he never attempted once to extirpate Whoring intirely: But like a true *Pastor* separated the clean Sheep from the unclean, and confin'd all the Courtezans to one Quarter of the City. It is true, he did attempt to moderate this Vice, and banish'd as many Courtezans as he thought exceeded the necessary Number; but he was soon convinc'd of the Error of his Computation, for *Sodomy*, and a thousand other unnatural Vices sprung up, which forc'd him soon to recal them, and has left us a remarkable Instance of the Vanity of such Attempts.

Let us now proceed to the Proof of our Proposition, in the first Part of which, it was asserted, That publick Whoring is neither so Criminal in itself, nor so Detrimental to the *Society*, as private Whoring.

Publick Whoring consists in lying with a certain Set of Women, who have shook off all Pretence to Modesty; and for such a Sum of Money, more or less, profess themselves always in a Readiness to be enjoy'd. The Mischief a Man does in this Case is intirely to himself; for with respect to the Woman, he does a laudable Action, in furnishing her with the Means of Subsistence, in the only, or at least most innocent way that she is capable of procuring it. The Damage he does to himself, is either with regard to his Health, or the Expence of Money, and may be consider'd under the same View as Drinking, with this considerable Advantage, that it restores us to that cool Exercise of our Reason, which Drinking tends to deprive us of. Indeed was there a Probability of a Woman's Amendment, and of her gaining a Livelihood by some honester Method, there might be some Crime in encouraging her to follow such a Profession: But the Minds of Women are observ'd to be so much corrupted by the Loss of Chastity, or rather by the Reproach they suffer upon that Loss, that they seldom or never change that Course of Life for the better; and if they should, they can never recover that good Name, which is so absolutely necessary to their getting a Maintenance in any honest Way whatever; and that nothing but meer Necessity obliges them to continue in that Course, is plain from this, That they themselves in Reality utterly abhor it: And indeed there appears nothing in it so very alluring and bewitching, especially to People who have that Inclination to Lewdness intirely extinguish'd, which is the only thing could possibly make it supportable,

The other Branch of Whoring, viz. *Private*, is of much worse Consequence; and a Man's Crime in this Case increases in proportion to the different Degree of Mischief done, if you consider his Crime with regard to the *Society*; for as to personal Guilt, Allowance ought to be made for the Increase of Temptation, which is very considerable in the Case of debauching *Married Women*; upon account of the Safety to the Aggressor, either with Respect to his Health, or the Charge, and, if that affects him, the Scandal of having a Bastard. On the other hand, the Injury done, is very considerable, as such an Action tends to corrupt a Woman's Mind, and destroy that mutual Love and Affection between Man and Wife, which is so necessary to both their Happiness. Besides, the Risque run of a Discovery, which at least ruins a Woman's Reputation, and destroys the Husband's Quiet; nay, where Virtue does not intirely give way, if it warps but ever so little, the Consequence is shockingly fatal: for tho' the good Man, suspicious of the Wife's Chastity, the Wife of the Gallant's Constancy, and the Gallant of the Husband's Watchfulness, by being a Check upon each other, may keep the Gate of Virtue shut; yet then even all Parties must be attended with a never-ceasing Misery, nor to be imagin'd, but by those who too fatally *feel it*.

The Crime of debauching young *Virgins* will appear much greater, if we consider that there is much more Mischief done, and the Temptation to do it much lessen'd by the fear of getting Children; which, in most Circumstances of Life, does a Man a deal of Prejudice, and keeps at least three Parts in four of our sober Youth from gratifying this violent Passion. Besides, the Methods that are necessary to be taken, before a Man can have such an Action in his Power, are in themselves Criminal; and it shows a certain Baseness of Mind to persuade a Woman, by a thousand solemn Vows and Protestations, into such a good Opinion of you, and Assurance of your Love to her, that she trusts you with all that is dear and near to her; and this with no other View but the Gratification of a present Passion, which might be otherwise vented, than at the certain Expence of her Ruin, and putting her under the Necessity of leading the Life of a *Publick Courtezan.*

From this general Consideration of Whoring, it is evident, that tho' all the several Species of it proceed from the same Cause, our natural Love and Passion for Women, yet they are very different in their Natures, and fully as distinct Crimes as those which proceed from our Love to Money, such as Murder, Shoplifting, &c. And I hope I have said enough to prove, that the Publick Part of it is by far the least Criminal, and least Detrimental to the *Society*; which of itself is a sufficient Motive for the *Legislature* to confine it to that Channel. I shall now proceed farther, and show, as I before propos'd, that the encouraging of Publick Whoring, will not only prevent most of the mischievous Effects of this Vice, but even lessen the Practice of Whoring in general, and reduce it to the narrowest Bounds which it can possibly be contain'd in.

When I talk'd of encouraging publick Whoring, I would be understood to mean, not only the erecting *Publick Stews*, as I at first hinted, but also the endowing them with such Privileges and Immunities, and at the same time giving such Discouragement to private Whoring, as may be most effectual to turn the general Stream of Lewdness into this common Channel.

I shall here lay down a Plan for this Purpose, which, tho' it may well serve to illustrate this Point, and make good the Proof of my present Argument, would doubtless receive infinite Improvement by coming through the Hands of a *National Senate*, whose august Body, being compos'd of *Spirituals* as well as *Temporals*, will, I hope, take into Consideration this Important Affair, which so nearly concerns both.

The Plan I would propose, is this: Let a hundred or more Houses be provided in some convenient Quarter of the City, and proportionably in every Country-Town, sufficient to contain two thousand Women: If a hundred are thought sufficient, let a hundred *Matrons* be appointed, one to each House, of Abilities and Experience enough to take upon them the Management of twenty Courtezans each, to see that they keep themselves neat and decent, and entertain Gentlemen after a civil and obliging Manner. For the encouragement of such *Matrons*, each House must be allow'd a certain Quantity of all sorts of Liquor, Custom and Excise free; by which Means they will be enabled to accommodate Gentlemen handsomely, without that Imposition so frequently met with in such Houses. Besides the hundred abovemention'd, there must be a very large House set apart for an Infirmary, and Provision made for two able Physicians, and four Surgeons at least. Lastly, there must be three Commissioners appointed to superintend the whole, to hear and redress Complaints, and to see that each House punctually observes such Rules and Orders as shall be thought necessary for the good Government of this Community. For the better Entertainment of all Ranks and Degrees of Gentlemen, we shall divide the twenty Women of each House into four Classes, who for their Beauty, or other Qualifications may justly challenge different Prices.

The first Class is to consist of eight, who may legally demand from each Visitant Half a Crown. The second Class to consist of six, whose fix'd Price may be a Crown. The third Class of four, at half a Guinea each. The remaining two make up the fourth Class, and are design'd for Persons of the first Rank, who can afford to pay a Guinea for the Elegancy of their Taste. To defray the Charges of this Establishment, will require but a very moderate Tax: For if the first Class pays but forty Shillings Yearly, and the rest in Proportion, it will amount to above 10,000 *l.* a Year, which will not only pay the Commissioners Salaries, Surgeons Chests, and other Contingencies, but likewise establish a good Fund for the Maintenance of Illegitimate Orphans and superannuated Courtezans.

For the better Government of this *Society*, it will be necessary that the Mistress have an absolute Command in her own House, and that no Woman be suffer'd to go abroad without her Leave. No Woman must be suffer'd to lie in, within the House; nor any young Children admitted under any Pretence. No Musick or Revelling to be allow'd in any Room, to the Disturbance of the rest. No Gentlemen disorderly or drunk, to be admitted at an unseasonable Hour, without the Consent of the Mistress: And, in case of Violence, she must be empower'd to call the Civil Aid.

For the *Society*'s Security in Point of Health, it must be order'd, That if any Gentleman complains of receiving an Injury, and the Woman, upon Search, be found tainted, without having discover'd it to the Mistress, she shall be stripp'd and cashier'd. But if a Woman discovers her Misfortune before any Complaint is made against her, she shall be sent to the *Infirmary*, and cured at the Publick Charge. No Woman that has been twice pox'd shall ever be re-admitted. *Note*, That three Claps shall be reckon'd equivalent to one Pox.

But as no *Society* ever fram'd a compleat Body of Laws at once, till overseen Accidents had taught them Foresight, we shall refer the farther Regulation of these Laws, with whatever new ones shall be thought necessary, to the *Wisdom* of the *Legislature*,

The *Publick Stews* being thus erected and govern'd by good and wholesome Laws, there remains nothing to compleat this Project, but that proper Measures be taken effectually to discourage all other Kinds of Whoring whatsoever. And here it is to be hoped, that those worthy *Gentlemen* of the *Society*, who have hitherto distinguish'd their *Zeal* to so little Purpose, will now exert themselves where they have so good a Prospect of Success; for altho' a poor Itinerant Courtezan could not by any Means be persuaded to starve at the Instigation of a *Reforming* Constable, yet a little *Bridewell* Rhetorick, or the Terrors of a Transportation, will soon convince her that she may live more comfortably and honestly in a *Publick Stew*. If there are any so foolish as to love Rambling better, or who are not qualify'd to please Gentlemen according to Law, they ought to be transported; for *Bridewell*, as it is now manag'd, only makes them poorer, and consequently lays them under a greater Necessity than ever of continuing Prostitutes.

Let us now suppose, for Brevity sake, that the *Publick Stews* are as much as possible favour'd and encourag'd, and that all the other Branches of this Vice have the utmost Rigour of the Laws exerted against them.

It now remains for me to show what Benefit the *Nation* would receive thereby, and how this Project would prevent or in any Degree alleviate those Mischiefs which I have mention'd to be the necessary Consequences of this Vice. As for any Objections that may be rais'd against me, either *Christian* or

Moral, I shall refer them to the Close of this Discourse.

First then, I say, the *Nation* would receive a general Benefit by having such a considerable Number of its most disorderly Inhabitants brought to live after a regular civiliz'd Manner. There is, one Year with another, a certain Number of young Women who arrive gradually, Step by Step, at the highest Degree of Impudence and Lewdness. These Women, besides their Incontinence, are commonly guilty of almost the whole Catalogue of immoral Actions: The Reason is evident; They are utterly abandon'd by their Parents, and thereby reduc'd to the last Degree of Shifting-Poverty; if their Lewdness cannot supply their Wants, they must have Recourse to Methods more criminal, such as *Lying*, *Cheating*, *open Theft*, &c. Not that these are the necessary Concomitants of Lewdness, or have the least Relation to it, as all *lewd Men of Honour* can testify; but the Treatment such Women meet with in the World, is the Occasion of it.

Those Females, who either by the Frigidity of their Constitutions, a lucky Want of Temptation, or any other Cause, have preserv'd their Chastity; and the Men, in general, Chaste or Unchaste, are so outrageous against these Delinquents, that they make no Distinction: all of them are branded with the same opprobrious Title, they are all treated with the same Contempt, all equally despis'd; so that let them be guilty of what other Crimes they please, they cannot add one Jot to the Shame they already undergo. Having thus remov'd the Fear of worldly Reproach, which is justly esteem'd the greatest *Bulwark* of *Morality*, it is no wonder if these Women, insensible of Shame, and prick'd on by Want, commit any Crimes, where they are not deter'd by the Fear of corporal Punishments. But the Case now will be quite alter'd; these Women, as soon as they have attain'd a competent Share of Assurance, and before they are pinch'd with the Extreme of Poverty, will enter themselves in some of the abovementioned Classes of profess'd Courtezans; where, instead of being necessarily dishonest, they will have more Inducements to Honesty than any other Profession whatsoever. The same Money defends, as well as it corrupts a *Prime Minister*: A *Churchman* takes Sanctuary in a Gown, and who dare accuse a Mitre of *Simony*? Accuse a *Colonel* of Injustice, he is try'd by his Board of *Officers*, and your Information is false, scandalous, and malicious. A *Lawyer* cheats you according to Law; and you may thank the *Physician*, if you live to complain of him. *Over-reaching* in Trade, is *prudent Dealing*; and *Mechanick Cunning*, is stiled *Handicraft*. Not so fares the poor Courtezan; if she commits but one ill Action, if, for Instance, she should circumvent a Gentleman of a *Snuff-Box*, she can hardly escape Detection; and the first Discovery ruins her; she is banish'd the *Publick Stews*, mark'd out for Infamy, and can have no better Prospect than a Transportation. On the other hand, the Motives to Honesty will be as great here as any where: It is natural for Mankind to regard chiefly the good Opinion of those with whom they converse, and to neglect that of Strangers: Now in this Community, Lewdness not being esteem'd a Reproach, but rather a Commendation, they will set a Value on their good Name, and stand as much upon the Puncto of Honour, as the rest of Mankind; being mov'd by the same commendable Emulation, and deter'd by greater, or at least more certain Punishments. Besides this Reformation in Point of Honesty, the Publick will receive another Benefit in being freed from those nocturnal Disorders, Quarrels and Brawlings, which are occasion'd by vagrant Punks, and the Number of private Brothels dispers'd throughout the City, to the great Disturbance of its sober Inhabitants.

We have already mention'd the *French Disease* as one of the worst Attendants upon Lewdness, and with good Reason; for in the Enjoyment of this Life, Health is the *sine qua non*: *i. e.* the greatest Happiness. And this Distemper has one Thing in it peculiarly inveterate, as if it came out of *Pandora's* worst Box; there is no other Disorder, but what at some Age, or in some particular Constitution, will abate of itself without the Application of Medicines; but this is such a busy restless Enemy, that unless resisted, he is never at a Stand, but gathers Strength every Day, to the utter Disquiet of the Patient. Now it is so evident that the *Publick Stews*, when well regulated, will prevent the Spreading of this Plague, that a prolix and tedious Proof of it would look like Declaiming. As this Disease has its Spring and Source entirely from publick Whoring, and from thence creeps into private Families; so it likewise receives continual Supplies and Recruits thro' the same Channel: When this Source is once dry'd up the Nation will naturally recover its pristine Health and Vigour: And this cannot fail to happen, if due Care be taken to keep the *Stews* free from Infection; for what young Fellow will be so industriously mad, as to take Pains to run his Head into an Apothecary's Shop, when he may with so much Ease and Conveniency, and without the Fear of a *Reforming Officer*, both secure his Health and gratify his Fancy with such a Variety of Mistresses.

'Tis true, the keeping of the *Publick Stews* so very safe, will appear a difficult Task, at first Sight; but not so if we consider the Case a little nearer. This Disease is propagated reciprocally from the Woman to the Man, and from the Man to the Woman; but the first is the most common for several Reasons: We are not like Cocks or Town-Bulls, who have a whole Seraglia of Females entirely and solely at their Devotion; on the contrary, one industrious Pains-taking Woman, who lays herself out that Way, is capable of satisfying several rampant Males; insomuch, that a select Number of Women get a handsome Livelihood by being able to oblige such a Number of Customers. Now, if but a few of these Women are unsound, they can infect a great many Men; whereas these Men have neither Power nor Inclination to infect the like Number of Women. I say, Inclination; for a Woman, to raise Money for the Surgeon's Fee, may counterfeit Pleasure when she really receives Pain; nay, she may even venture to complain of being hurt: for the Man will attribute the Pain he gives her, either to her Chastity, or his own Vigour; not dreaming, perhaps, that he has molested a *Shanker*. This a Female may do, as being only passive in the Affair, but a Man must have real Fancy and Inclination before he is qualify'd to enter upon Action: And how far this Fancy to Woman may be cool'd by a stinging *Gonorrhœa*, I leave the experienc'd Reader to judge; and whether a Man won't rather employ his Thoughts upon his *round Diet*, *i. e.* Pills, how to digest 2 at Night, and 3 in the Morning; what Conveyance to find out when poach'd Eggs grow nauseous, and how to preserve his Linnen from being speckled; with a Thousand other Particulars that occur to a Man in this Distress: but these are sufficient, with the Assistance of a *Cordee*, to *bridle* any moderate Passion. So that from the whole we may safely draw this Conclusion; That since the Men are so seldom guilty of transgressing in this Kind, the spreading of this Distemper must be owing to the Neglect of Cure in the Women. Now the *Publick Stews* will be so regulated, that a Woman cannot possibly conceal her Misfortune long; nay, it will be highly her Interest to make the first Discovery; so that whatever Damage the *Society* may sustain at first, when Claps are most current, it will be soon repair'd, and this Distemper, in Time, entirely rooted out. But of this enough.

The next Thing that comes to be consider'd in this Vice, is the Expence it occasions, and the Neglect of worldly Business, by employing so much of our Time and Thoughts; for let a Man have ever so much Business, it can't stop the Circulation of his Blood, or prevent the Seminal Secretion: for Sleeping or

Waking, the *Spermaticks* will do their Office, tho' a Man's Thoughts may be so much employ'd about other Affairs, that he cannot attend to every minute Titillation. A Man of Pleasure, indeed, may make this copulative Science his whole Study; and, by Idleness and Luxury, may prompt Nature that Way, and spur up the Spirits to Wantonness: but then his Constitution will be the sooner tired; for the Animal Spirits being exhausted by this Anticipation, his Body must be weaken'd, and his Nerves relax'd; neither will his irregular effeminate Life assist them in recovering their former Force. Besides, those Parts which more particularly suffer the Violence of this Exercise, are liable to many Accidents; and Men of Pleasure, though otherwise pretty healthy, are often troubled with Gleets and Weaknesses, either by a former Ulceration of the *Prostrates*, or else some violent Over-straining, which occasions this Relaxation. These Men, 'tis true, will talk very lusciously of Women; but, pretend what they please, they can never have that burning Desire which they had formerly, when their Vessels were in full Vigour. The Truth is, their Lust lies chiefly in their Brain, kept alive by the Impression of former Ideas, which are not so easily rubb'd out as the Titillation which created them; and this Passion comes to be so diminished, that, in Time, it changes its Residence from the *Glans Penis* to the *Glandula Penealis*. A Man of Business, on the contrary, or one who leads a sober regular Life, will seldomer be attack'd by these wanton Fits, but then they will come with double the Violence; for though it is a common received Opinion, that the longer a Man refrains, the better he is able to refrain, yet it is only true in one Sense, and amounts to no more than this: That if a Man has been able, for such and such Reasons, to curb this Passion, for Instance, a Month, he will, if the same Reasons hold, and without an additional Temptation, be able to curb it a Month longer; but, nevertheless, he may have Desires much stronger than a Man who, for want of these Motives to Abstinence, gratifies them every Day. If there are some Men of a particular Constitution, whose puny Desires may be easily block'd up with the Assistance of *three small Buttons*: or else endow'd with such an extraordinary Strength of Reason, that they can master the most *rampant* Sallies of this raging Passion; I heartily congratulate their happy Conquest, but have nothing more to do with them at present, the *Publick Stews* not being design'd for such: I am here speaking of those Men of Business, who, notwithstanding their Abstinence or the Regularity of their Lives, are sometimes prevailed upon to quench these amorous Heats; and, I say, in such Men the Passion is much stronger than in Men of Pleasure, and that their

Abstinence contributes to heighten the Violence of the Desire, and make it the more irresistible: for the Fancy not being cloy'd with too frequent Enjoyment, presently takes fire; and the *Spermaticks*, not being weaken'd with forc'd Evacuations, are in their full Vigour, and give the Nerves a most exquisite Sensation: so that upon the least toying with an alluring Wench, the Blood-Vessels are ready to start; and to use *Othello*'s Words, *The very Sense aches at her.*

Now, what shall this Man do, when he has once taken the Resolution to make himself easy? He must either venture upon the Publick, where, it is Odds, he may meet with a Mischance that will either drain his Pocket, and make him unfit for any Business, at least without Doors; or else he must employ both his Time and Rhetoric, and perhaps too his Purse, in deluding some modest Girl; which, besides the Loss of Time in carrying on such an Intrigue, is apt to give the Head such an amorous Turn as is quite inconsistent with Business, and may probably lead a Man into After-Expences, which at first he never dreamt of.

Now to remedy all these Inconveniences, the *Publick Stews* will be always ready and open, where a Man may regulate his Expences according to his Ability, from Half a Crown to a Guinea; and that too without endangering his Health: And besides, which is chiefly to be consider'd, if a Man should be overtaken with a sudden Gust of Lechery, it will be no Hindrance to him even in the greatest Hurry of Business, for a ready and willing Mistress will ease him in the twinkling of an Eye, and he may prosecute his Affairs with more Attention than ever, by having his Mind entirely freed and disengag'd from those troublesome Ideas which always accompany a wanton Disposition of the Body. But to proceed:

Another ill Consequence of Whoring, is the Tendency it has to dispeople a Nation; and that both by the Destruction of Illegitimate Infants, and by ruining young Men's Constitutions so much, that, when they marry, they either beget no Children, or such as are sickly and short-liv'd. The first of these, indeed, is almost unavoidable, especially in modest Women, who will be guilty of this Cruelty as long as Female Chastity carries that high Reputation along with it, which it really deserves: However, in common Women, it may and will be, in a great measure, prevented by this Scheme; for every profess'd Courtezan, that is legally licens'd, will have an Apartment allotted her in the Infirmary when she is ready to lie in, and will be obliged to take Care of her Child; by which means a considerable Number of Infants will be reared up, that otherwise might probably have perish'd. Besides, there are a great many ordinary Girls, such as Servant-Maids, who are chiefly mov'd to this Action, by the fear of losing their Services, and wanting Bread. Now this handsome Provision that is made for them, will be a great Inducement for such to enter themselves in the *Stews*, rather than commit such an unnatural Action, especially when the Discovery is Death.

Let us now consider the Affair of Matrimony. Since the World is now no longer in a State of Nature, but form'd into several Societies independent of one another, and these Societies again divided into several Ranks and Degrees of Men, distinguish'd by their Titles and Possessions, which descend from Father to Son; it is very certain that Marriage is absolutely necessary, not only for the regular Propagation of the *Species*, and their careful Education, but likewise for preserving that Distinction of Rank among Mankind, which otherwise would be utterly lost and confounded by doubtful Successions. And it is no less certain and indisputable, that all Sorts and Kinds of Debauchery whatever are Enemies to this State, in so far as they impair the natural Vigour of the Constitution, and weaken the very Springs of Love.

This necessary Passion is, indeed, of such a ticklish Nature, that either too much or too little of it is equally prejudicial, and the *Medium* is so hard to hit, that we are apt to fall into one of the Extremes. We are naturally *furnish'd* with an extraordinary *Stock* of Love; and, by the *Largeness* of the Provision, it looks as if Nature had made some Allowance for *Wear and Tear*. If young Men were to live intirely chaste and sober, without blunting the Edge of their Passions, the first Fit of Love would turn their Brains Topsy-turvy, and we should have the Nation pestered with Love-Adventures and Feats of Chivalry: By the time a *Peer's* Son came to be Sixteen, he would be in danger of turning Knight-Errant, and might possibly take a Cobler's Daughter for his *Dulcinea*; and who knows but a sprightly young *Taylor* might turn an *Orlando Furioso*, and venture his Neck to carry off a Lady of Birth and Fortune. In short, there are so many Instances every day of these ruinous disproportion'd Matches, notwithstanding our present Intemperance, that we may justly conclude, if the Nation was in a State of perfect Sobriety, no Man could answer for the Conduct of his Children.

It must, indeed, be confess'd, as Matters now stand, the Excess of Chastity is not so much to be fear'd as the other Extreme of Lewdness, tho' there are

Instances of both; and many Fathers, now living, would gladly have seen their Sons fifty times in a *Stew*, rather than see them so unfortunately married. The other Extreme is equally, or rather more dangerous, as it is more common; for most young Men give too great a Loose to their Passions, and either quite destroy their Inclination to Matrimony, or make their Constitutions incapable of answering the Ends of that State.

To avoid therefore these two dangerous Extremes, we have erected the *Publick Stews*, which every considerate Man must allow to be that Golden Mean so much desired: For, in the first Place, we avoid the Inconvenience of too strict a Chastity. When a Man has gained some Experience by his Commerce in the *Stews*, he is able to form a pretty good comparative Judgment of what he may expect from the highest Gratifications of Love; he finds his Ideas of Beauty strangely alter'd after Enjoyment, and will not be hurry'd into an unsuitable Match by those romantick chimerical Notions of Love, which possess the Minds of unexperienced Youth, and make them fancy that Love alone can compleat the Happiness of a married State. But this will be so readily granted, that I shan't insist upon it farther.

In the next Place, the *Publick Stews* will prevent the ill Effects of excessive Lewdness, by preserving Men's Constitutions so well, that although they may defer Matrimony some time for their special Advantage, yet they will have a sufficient Stock of Desire left to perswade them, one time or other, to quit the Gaiety of a Single Life: and when they do marry, they will be able to answer all the Ends and Purposes of that State as well, and rather better, than if they had lived perfectly chaste.

This may seem a bold Proposition, but the Proof of it is nevertheless obvious. However, to proceed methodically, there are three Ways by which lewd young Men destroy their natural Vigour, and render themselves Impotent: First, By Manufriction, *alias* Masturbation. Secondly, By too frequent and immoderate Enjoyment. And, Lastly, By contracting Venereal Disorders, as Claps or Poxes.

The first lewd Trick that Boys learn, is this Manual Diversion; and when they have once got the knack of it, they seldom quit it till they come to have actual Commerce with Women: The Safety, Privacy, Convenience, and Cheapness of this Gratification are very strong Motives, and chiefly persuade young Men to continue the Practice of it.

If these Pollutionists were so abstemious as to wait the ordinary Calls of Nature, this Action, however unnatural, would be no more prejudicial, when prudently managed, than common Copulation; but, instead of this, they are every Day committing *Rapes* upon their own Bodies; and though they have neither real Inclination nor Ability to attack a Woman, yet they can attack themselves, and supply all these Defects by the Agility of their Wrists; by which means they so weaken their Genitals, and accustom them to this violent Friction, that, tho' they have frequently Evacuations without an Erection, yet the common and ordinary Sensation which Females afford to those Parts, is not able of itself to promote this Evacuation: so that they are impotent to all Intents and Purposes of Generation.

To put a Stop therefore to these clandestine Practices, and prevent young Men from laying *violent Hands* upon themselves, we must have Recourse to the *Publick Stews*, which cannot fail to have the desired Effect: For which of these private Practitioners can be so brutish, as to prefer this boyish solitary Amusement before the actual Embraces of a fine Woman, when they can proceed with the same Convenience, Safety, and Privacy in the one, as well as the other.

In the next Place, Men are often weaken'd, and sometimes contract almost incurable Gleets by too frequent and immoderate Enjoyment. This seldom or never happens but in private Whoring, when some particular Mistress has made such a strong Impression upon a Man's Fancy, that he exerts himself in an extraordinary Manner beyond his natural Ability, and thereby contracts a Seminal Weakness, which is generally more difficult to cure than a virulent Running. Now this Danger will be pretty well remov'd by the Encouragement given to *Publick Whoring*, which, as I shall show more particularly hereafter, will divert Men's Minds, and turn their Thoughts very much from private Intrigues: And it will be readily granted me, that no such Excess is to be fear'd in *Publick Stews*; where a Man only acting out of a general Principle of Love to the whole Sex, will be in no Danger of proceeding any farther than he is prompted by Nature, and the particular Disposition of his Body at that Time.

As for the third Cause of Impotency, the Venereal Disease, we have already prov'd that this Institution of the *Stews* is the best and surest Remedy against it; and shall only observe here how happily this Project provides against the various ill Effects of Lewdness, in whatever Light we consider them.

Thus, I think, the first Part of my Proposition pretty well clear'd, *viz.* That the *Publick Stews* will preserve Mens Constitutions so well, that they will have a sufficient Stock of corporal Ability, and consequently Inclination left to persuade them, sooner or later, to enter into the Marriage-State.

I say farther, that these Men, having thus preserv'd their Constitution, will answer all the Intents and Purposes of that State, rather better than if they had lived perfectly chaste.

When a Man and a Woman select one another out of the whole Species, it is not merely for Propagation; nay, that is generally the least in their Thoughts: What they chiefly have in View, is to pass the Remainder of their Lives happily together, to enjoy the soft Embraces and mutual Endearments of Love; to divide their Joys and Griefs; to share their Pleasures and Afflictions; and, in short, to make one another as happy as possible. As for Children, they come of Course, and of Course are educated according to their Parents Abilities.

Now all these Enjoyments depending upon the mutual Affection of these two, Man and Wife; whenever this Affection fails, either in the Woman or the Man, that Marriage is unhappy, and all the good Ends and Designs of this State entirely frustrated. To give the Women their Due, they must have the Preference in Point of Constancy; their Passions are not so easily rais'd, nor so suddenly fix'd upon any particular Object: but when this Passion is once rooted in Women, it is much stronger and more durable than in Men, and rather increases than diminishes, by enjoying the Person beloved. Whether it is that Women receive as much Love as they part with, and that the Love they receive is not entirely lost, but takes Root again by Conception; whereas what a Man parts with never affects him further, than just the Pleasure he receives at the time of parting with it: or whether this Difference is owing to the different Turn of Mens Fancies, which are more susceptible of fresh Impressions from every handsome Face they meet, or perhaps that their Heads are so much employ'd in worldly Affairs, that they only take Love *en passant* to get rid of a present Uneasiness, whereas Women make it the whole Business of their Lives: Whatever the Reason is, I say, it is experimentally true, that a Woman has but a very *slippery Hold* of a Man's Affections after Enjoyment. Let us see therefore which of these two, the chaste or the experienc'd Man, will be least liable to this Failure of Affection, and consequently which of the two will make the best married Man.

The first great Cooler of a Man's Affections after Marriage, is the Disparity of the Match. When a Man has married entirely for Love, and to the apparent Detriment of his worldly Affairs, as soon as the first Flash of it is over, he can't help reflecting upon the Woman as the Cause, and, in some Sense, the Author of his Misfortunes; This naturally begets a Coldness and Indifference, which, by Degrees, turns to an open Dislike. Now it is these sorts of Marriages that chaste Men are always in danger of falling into, as I have already proved; neither is there any effectual Way to convince a Man of this Folly, and secure him against it, but by giving him some Experience in Love-Affairs. Again, as chaste Men seldom marry for any thing but sheer Love, so they have framed to themselves such high extravagant Notions of the Raptures they expect to possess in the Marriage-Bed, that they are mightily shocked at the Disappointment. A chaste unexperienc'd Man is strangely surprized, that those bewitching Charms should make such a faint Impression upon him after a thorow Perusal; he can scarce believe that the Woman is still possessed of the same Charms which transported him formerly; he fancies he has discover'd abundance of little Faults and Imperfections, and attributes his growing Dislike to this Discovery, not dreaming that this Alteration is entirely in himself, and not in the Object of Desire, which remains still the same. The Truth is, when a Man is full fraught with Love, and that his Pulse beats high for Enjoyment, this peccant Love-Humour falls down upon the Eye, which may be observ'd at such a time to be full brisk and sparkling: 'Tis then the Beauty of every Feature is magnified. and *Parthenope* is no less than a Goddess. But when this dazzling Humour is drawn downwards by a Revulsion, as in the Case of Marriage, a Man's Eyes are perfectly open'd; and though they may look languid, sunk, and environ'd with blueish Circles, yet he actually sees much better than before; for *Parthenope* will now appear to him a Mortal, such as she really is, divested of all those false Glosses and Appearances.

The chaste Man is surprized at this Change; he is apt to lay the Fault upon the Woman, and generally fixes his Affections on some other Female, who, he imagines, is free from those Faults: then farewel happy Wedlock. The experienc'd Man, on the contrary, has try'd several Women; he finds they all agree in one Particular, and that after a Storm of Love there always succeeds a Calm: When he enters into Matrimony, he is prepar'd against any Disappointments of that Nature, and is ready to make Allowance for those

Faults and Imperfections which are inseparable from Human Kind. This is so true, that Women have establish'd a Maxim, that Rakes make the best Husbands; for they are very sensible how difficult it is to monopolize a Man's Affections; that he will have his Curiosity about those Affairs satisfied one time or other: And tho' this Experience is useful before Marriage, it is very dangerous afterwards.

Besides, to compleat the Happiness of the Marriage-State, or indeed to make it tolerably easy, there must be some Agreement in the Temper, Humour, and Disposition of the two Parties concern'd. If, for Instance, the Man can't endure the Sight of a *Metropolis*, and the Woman can't enjoy herself out of it; if the Man is grave, serious, and an Enemy to all jocular Merriment, when his Wife is a profess'd Lover of Mirth and Gaiety, these two can never agree: Differences will arise every Day, and Differences in Wedlock are as hard to reconcile as those in Religion: We may guess at the Reason from a parallel Instance.

After the Revocation of the Edict of *Nantz*, several Protestant Gentlemen were shut up in the *Bastile* at *Paris*, where they liv'd constantly together for a considerable Time: They made an Observation, during their Stay there, That whenever the least Difference or Dispute happen'd amongst them, it was never reconciled till some time after their Enlargement; because, said they, altho' we were Yoke-Fellows in Affliction, yet never being out of one another's Company, our Animosities were always kept up warm, for want of a little Absence to cool them. It is the same Case with Matrimony; and People ought to be particularly careful to chuse a Wife as nearly of their own Temper as possible.

Now this Consideration never enters into the Head of a chaste unexperienc'd Man, he is so infatuated with personal Love, that he imagines his whole future Happiness depends upon the Possession of such a Shape, or such a Composition of Features; when he is disappointed in this, how much will it add to his Chagrin, to find himself yoked for Life to a Woman whose Temper is quite opposite to his own, and consequently whose Satisfaction is quite inconsistent with his? We may guess the Sequel; separate Beds, separate Maintenance, and all the whole Train of Conjugal Misfortunes. In short, let us consider Matrimony under what View we please, we shall still find that the experienc'd Man will make the best Husband, and answer all the Ends of Marriage much better than a Man who lives perfectly chaste to his Wedding-

Day.

Thus, we see, by this happy Regulation of the *Publick Stews*, that Whoring, instead of being an Enemy to Matrimony, will advance and promote the Interest of it as much as possible.

We come to the last great Point propos'd, *viz.* that this Project of the *Publick Stews* will prevent, as much a possible, the debauching of modest Women, and thereby reduce Whoring to the narrowest Bounds in which it can possibly be contain'd.

To illustrate this Matter, we must step a little back to consider the Constitution of Females, while they are in a State of Innocence; and when we have taken a View of the Fortifications which Nature has made to preserve their Chastity, we shall find out the Reason why it is so often surrender'd, and be the better able to provide for its Defence.

Every Woman, who is capable of Conception, must have those Parts which officiate so framed, that they may be able to perform whatever is necessary at that Juncture. Now, to have those Parts so rightly adapted for the Use which Nature design'd them, it is requisite that they should have a very quick Sensation, and, upon the Application of the *Male-Organ*, afford the Woman an exquisite Pleasure; for without this extravagant Pleasure in Fruition, the recipient Organs could never exert themselves to promote Conception as they now do, in such an extraordinary Manner: The whole *Vagina*, as one continu'd *Sphincter*, contracting and embracing the *Penis*, while the *Nymphæ* and adjacent Islands have their particular Emissions at that critical Minute, either as a Vehicle to lubricate the Passage, or else to incorporate with the Masculine Injection: Add to this, that the *Fallopian Tubes* put themselves in a proper Posture to receive the impregnating Fluid, and convey it, as is suppos'd, to the *Ovaria*. Now it is hard to imagine, that so many alert Members, which can exert themselves in such a lively Manner on this Occasion, should be at all other Times in a State of perfect Tranquillity; for, besides that Experience teaches us the contrary, this handsome Disposition would be entirely useless, if Nature had not provided a prior Titillation, to provoke Women at first to enter upon Action; and all our late Discoveries, in Anatomy, can find out no other Use for the *Clitoris*, but to whet the Female Desire by its frequent Erections; which are, doubtless, as provoking as those of the *Penis*, of which it is a perfect Copy, tho' in Miniature.

In short, there requires no more to convince us of the Violence of Female Desire, when raised to a proper height, but only to consider, what a terrible Risque a Woman runs to gratify it. Shame and Poverty are look'd upon as Trifles, when they come in Competition with this predominating Passion. But altho' it must be allow'd, that all Women are liable to these amorous Desires, yet, the Variety of Constitutions will make a considerable Difference; for as in some Men the *Olfactory, Auditory,* or *Optick* Nerves, are not so brisk and lively as in others, so there are some Women who have the Nerves of their *Pudenda* more lively, and endow'd with a much quicker Sensation than others. Now, whether this Difference is owing to the Formation of the Nerves, or to the different Velocity of the Blood circulating thro' those Parts, or whether it is owing to the different Quantity, or perhaps Acrimony, of that Fluid which is separated from the Blood by the *Nymphæ*, and other titillating Glands: I say, from whencesoever this Difference proceeds, according to the Degree of this Sensation, we may venture to pronounce a Woman more or less in their own Nature Chaste.

To counterballance this violent natural Desire, all young Women have strong Notions of Honour carefully inculcated into them from their Infancy. Young Girls are taught to hate a *Whore*, before they know what the Word means; and when they grow up, they find their worldly Interest entirely depending upon the Reputation of their Chastity. This Sense of Honour and Interest, is what we may call artificial Chastity; and it is upon this Compound of natural and artificial Chastity, that every Woman's real actual Chastity depends.

As for Instance, some Women are naturally more Chaste, or rather, to speak properly, less Amorous than others, and at the same time have very strict Notions of Honour. Such Women are almost impregnable, and may be compar'd to Towns strongly fortify'd both by Art and Nature, which, without Treachery, are safe from any sudden Attacks, and must be reduc'd by long and regular Sieges, such as few Men have the Patience or Resolution to go thro' with.

Other Women, again, have the same Value for their Reputation, and stand as much upon the Puncto of Honour; but then they are naturally of a very sanguine amorous Disposition. A Woman of this Class may not unjustly be compar'd to a Town well garrison'd, but whose mutinous unruly *Inhabitants* are strongly inclin'd to revolt and *let in* the Enemy. Such Women, it's true, by extraordinary Care and Vigilance may suppress these Mutinies; and Honour may for a long while keep Inclination under, but yet they are never perfectly safe; there are certain Times and Seasons, certain unguarded Hours, when Honour and Interest are lull'd asleep, and Love has got the entire Ascendant. Besides, altho' we allow Love and Honour to be pretty equal Combatants, nay even granting, that in a *Pitch'd Battle*, when they have muster'd up all their Forces, Honour will have the Advantage, and quell Inclination; yet, in the Course of a long *Civil War*, it is Odds but Love one Time or other obtains a Victory, which is sure to be decisive: for Inclination has this unlucky Advantage over Honour, that, instead of being weaken'd, it grows stronger by Subjection; and, like *Camomile*, the more it is press'd down and kept under, the sturdier it grows; or, like *Antæus*, it receives fresh Vigour from every Defeat, and rises the brisker the oftener it is thrown. Whereas Honour once routed never rallies; nay, the least *Breach* in Female Reputation is irreparable; and a *Gap* in Chastity, like a *Chasm* in a young Tree, is every Day a *Widening*. Besides, Honour and Interest require a long Chain of solid Reasoning before they can be set in Battle-Array: Whereas Inclination is presently under Arms, the Moment Love has pitch'd his *Standard*: For, as we find that the least wanton Glance of a Lady's Eye quickly alarms a Man's Animal Spirits, and puts the whole Body Corporate into an unruly Ferment; so, doubtless, the Female Imagination is at least equally alert: and in such a sudden Scuffle betwixt Love and Honour, it is ten to one but the Enemy *enters*; for the *Gate* of Chastity, like the *Temple* of *Janus*, always stands *open* during these Conflicts. It must indeed be granted, that if the Loss of Honour was immediately to succeed the Loss of Chastity, the Virtue of these Women would be much stronger than it is; but they flatter themselves with the Hopes of Secrecy, and fancy that they have found out an Expedient to purchase Pleasure without the Expence of Reputation; by this Means Honour is reconciled to Inclination, or at best made to stand Neuter; and then the Consequence is very obvious. In short, a wanton Woman of Honour may withstand a great many Attacks, and possibly defend her Chastity to the very last; but yet she is every Day in danger of being surpriz'd, and at best will make but a very precarious Defence.

A third Sort of Women, the very Reverse of the preceding, have neither Honour nor Inclination; that is to say, they have neither the one nor the other to an equal Degree with the rest of the Sex. These Kinds of Women, who put a slighter Value than ordinary upon their Characters, are generally, in their Circumstances, either above the World or below it; for when a Woman has her Interest and Fortune depending upon her Reputation, as all the middle Rank of Womankind have, she is a Woman of Honour of course. Interest, indeed, is inseparable from Female Honour, nay, it is the very Foundation of it; and Honour and Interest, when they are consider'd as Guardians to Chastity, are synonimous Terms. The bare Puncto of Honour, when abstracted from Interest, would prove but a small Rub to Women in their eager Pursuit of Pleasure: Thus we see the Conduct of a Maiden Lady, how much more circumspect it is whilst her Fortune in Marriage is depending, than afterwards, when that Point of Interest is secured by a Husband; for all marry'd Women are above the World, in so far as they are out of the Reach of any Suspicions or Surmises, or even a Probability of Incontinence; and since they are not liable to be detected by Pregnancy, there's no other Sort of Conviction able to prejudice them, but downright ocular Demonstration: Which seems to be the Reason why so many of them take such Liberties, as if they were of *Falstaff's* Opinion, when he said, *Nothing but Eyes confutes me.* Female Honour, therefore, being so nearly ally'd and closely annex'd to worldly Interest, we must confine this Class of Women to two Sorts: First, those whose Fortunes are independent, and above being influenc'd by the Censure of the World; and, secondly, those who are far below the World, that they either escape its Censure, or else are incapable of being hurt by it. The first Sort lie under this Disadvantage, that let their natural Chastity be ever so great, the smallest Spark of Desire is capable of being blown up and rais'd to a considerable Pitch; whereas, when a Woman is once arriv'd to Maturity, that Portion of Honour which she has acquir'd, is with Difficulty preserv'd, and at best is incapable of any Improvement. The second Sort are equally liable to have their Passions rais'd, however low they may be naturally, and besides lie under this farther Disadvantage, that tho' they cannot promote their Interest by preserving their Chastity, yet, if they have the least Spark of Beauty, they will find their Account sufficiently in parting with it. The Virtue, indeed, of this Class of Women, seems chiefly to depend upon the Degree of Beauty which they stand possess'd of; for if they have Charms sufficient to provoke young Men to be at any tolerable Pains and Cost, their Chastity can never hold out long, but must infallibly surrender.

The fourth and last Kind of Women we shall mention, are those who have a very moderate Share of Honour, join'd to a very amorous Constitution.

The Virtue of these Women is entirely defenceless; and, as soon as a Man has removed that little timorous Coyness, which is natural to young Women in their first Attempts, he may proceed with Confidence, and conclude the Breach to be practicable; for whatever Resistance he meets with afterwards, will only enhance the Pleasure of Conquest. Most Women, indeed, let them be ever so fully resolv'd to comply, make as great a Shew of Resistance as they can conveniently counterfeit; and this the Sex would pass upon the World for a kind of innate Modesty: but it is very easily accounted for.

As soon as Women have entertain'd any Degree of Love, they make it their whole Study to raise and maintain an equal Degree of Passion in the Men; and they are very sensible how far the bare Appearance of Modesty will prevail to render them amiable. The Pain they suffer in smothering their Desires, is fully recompenced by that secret Pleasure which a Lover's Eagerness gives them, because they esteem it a Proof both of the Sincerity and Violence of his Passion. A Woman is not, without some Reason, afraid, lest a Man's Love should diminish after Enjoyment, and would gladly bribe his After-Love, by the great Value she seems to put upon her Chastity before she makes him a Present of it.

Besides, not to mention the actual Pleasure a Woman receives in Struggling, it is a Justification of her in the Eye of the Man, and a kind of *Salvo* to her Honour and Conscience, that she never did fully comply, but was in a manner forced into it. This is the plain natural Reason why most Women refuse to *surrender* upon *Treaty*, and why they delight so much in being *storm'd*.

Having thus taken a cursory View of the Sex, in their several Classes, and according to their several Circumstances, we may conclude, preferring Truth to Complaisance, that by far the greater Part of Womenkind hold their Virtue very precariously; and that Female Chastity is, in its own Nature, built upon a very *ticklish* Foundation.

Hudibras has ludicrously plac'd the Seat of Male-Honour, in the Posteriors, whereby it is secur'd from any Attack in Front; but Female Honour, notwithstanding the apparent Safety of the Situation, like a Debtor's House upon the Verge of two Counties, is liable to be attack'd both Ways; *à parte* ante, & *à parte* post,

That the Seat of Honour in Females has this double Aspect, like *Janus bifrons*, and consequently that it is two Ways accessible, has already been taken Notice of by almost all the *Writers* upon this Subject; but it is worth remarking here, that *Lycurgus* had an Eye to it when he modelled the *Spartan* Petticoat; for tho' the Warmth of the Climate obliged the Women to be very open in that Part of their Dress, insomuch that, if we believe *Plutarch*, in his Comparison of *Numa* and *Lycurgus*, the Habit which the Maidens of *Laconia* wore came but to their Knees, and was open on both Sides, so that as they walked their Thighs appear'd bare; yet this wise *Law-giver* would not permit them to make the least Aperture, either in the fore or hind Part of that Garment; rightly judging, that those two sacred *Avenues* to a Maid's Honour ought to be guarded with the utmost Caution.

For this same Reason the upright Posture of the Body has always been esteem'd the most decent; and it has ever been the Mode, in all Countries, for Ladies to cursey instead of bowing: for, tho' a Female-Bow, might seem a modest and coy Reclension of the Body, with regard to the Person saluted, yet it would occasion a very indecent Projection to those who should happen to be behind; especially since that dangerous Fashion of *Postern-Plackets* has crept into the *European* Petticoat.

But to return to our present Argument, the Design of which was to prove the following *Syllogism*.

The only way to preserve Female Chastity, is to prevent the Men from laying Siege to it: And this Project of the *Publick Stews* is the only Way to prevent Mens laying Siege to it: Therefore this Project is the only Way to preserve Female Chastity.

The former Part of the Proposition is, I hope, sufficiently proved. It is, indeed, evident, from the bare Consideration of the Nature of Females, that if the Men are suffer'd to go on, as they now do, in the Pursuit of Pleasure, there is no possible Way can be found out, effectually, to secure the Virtue of any one Woman of any Rank, or in any Station of Life. If a Woman is handsome, she has the more Tryals to undergo; if homely, and for that Reason seldom attack'd, the Novelty of the Address makes the greater Impression: If she is married, it is odds but there's a Failure at home, and habitual Pleasures are not easily foregone, especially when they may be enjoy'd with Safety: If a Maid, her unexperienc'd Virgin-Heart is capable of any Impression: If she is rich, Ease and Luxury make the Blood run mad; and Love, if high-dieted, is ungovernable: If poor, she will be the easier bribed, when Love and Avarice jointly must be gratified.

In short, to sum up all, there is in the Passion of Love a certain fatal *Crisis*, to which all Womenkind are capable of being wrought-up: The Difference of Virtue consisting only in this, that it is very hard to work a virtuous Woman up to this *Crisis*, and requires a very unlucky Concurrence of Circumstances: Whereas a Woman without a good Stock of Virtue, must have an unaccountable Series of good Fortune if she escapes. But, virtuous or not virtuous, when this Passion is once rais'd to the *critical* Height, it is absolutely irresistible.

Since therefore Female Virtue cannot effectually be secured, but by preventing the Men from laying Siege to it, it remains for us to examine, if this Prevention can be effected by any other Method than that of erecting the *Publick Stews*, and whether or no when erected, they will have the desired Effect.

That young Men, in a good State of Health, have their Desires towards Women much stronger, and more violent, than for the Enjoyment of any thing else in this Life, is a Truth not to be contested. And it is likewise as certain, that young Men will gratify these Desires, unless the *Legislature* can affix such a Penalty to the Commission of the Fact, that the Apprehension of the Penalty may give their Minds more Uneasiness, than refraining from the Gratification.

Now there are but three Things which Men fear in this Life, *viz.* Shame, Poverty, and Bodily Pain, and consequently but three Sorts of Punishments, which the *Legislature* can inflict. The first of these, indeed, might be omitted; for Shame is so very little in the Power of the Laws, that it hardly deserves the Name of a Penalty. If the Pillory, and such like infamous Punishments, are more terrible for the Shame that attends them, than for the bodily Pain, it is not because such a Posture of a Man's Body, with his Neck through a Hole, is in itself ignominious, or that any Law can make it so; but because it publishes to the World, that a Man has been prov'd to commit such a certain Action, in its own Nature scandalous, which he is asham'd to have thus publickly made known. The truth is, "Honour and Dishonour being only the different

Opinions of Mankind, as to the Good or Evil of any Action; and these Opinions in the Mind arising, as Dr. *Clarke* well observes, from the natural Fitness or Unfitness of the Actions themselves, cannot be alter'd or determin'd by any *Secular Force*." And that they are entirely out of the Power of the *Legislature*, is evident in the Instance of *Duelling*; where a Man often receives Honour for a *Breach* of the Law, nay is forced to *break* it in *Defence* of his Honour.

The utmost Scandal, therefore, which the Laws can affix to any Action, is to make a full and open Publication of the Fact: Now it is evident that this Publication cannot have a sufficient Influence over Mens Minds to deter them from Wenching, a Crime which meets with so favourable a Reception in the Eye of the World, that young Men are not asham'd to boast of it.

We must have Recourse then to a Fine, or Corporal Punishment, or perhaps both. If it is a Fine, it must be one of these three sorts; either a certain determinate Sum for every Offence, or, to make it fall more equally, such a certain Portion of a Man's whole Substance, or else it must be such a Sum as the Jury shall think sufficient to repair the Woman's Damages. The first is impracticable because of its Inequality, with regard to Mens different Fortunes. The second would punish none but Men of Fortune. And the third, in many Cases, would be impossible; for Women are often ruin'd by such as have it not in their power to make them amends. But granting that a Fine could be so happily contriv'd as to affect all Men equally in their several Stations of Life; and let us suppose this Fine considerable enough, for so it must be, to deter any moderate-spirited Man: yet still we lie under a manifest Dilemma as to the Point of Proof; for if the Proof is to depend upon the Evidence of Eye-Witnesses, none but Fools will be convicted; and let a Man be ever so indiscreet, he that swears to *rem in re* must have good Eyes, and be a good Swearer withal. If, on the other hand, a Man is to be convicted upon the sole Evidence of the Woman, we run into greater Inconveniences: for either a Woman is to be recompenced for the Injury she has received, or not; if not, there is no modest Woman of common Sense, but will chuse much rather to conceal her Weakness, than expose it in publick Court so much to her own Prejudice; and this too upon the sole Motive of doing Prejudice to a Man, for whom, in all Probability, she still retains an Affection: So that no Man would be accus'd but by such sort of Women as the Law can never intend to favour or countenance.

And if the Woman is to receive this Fine, either in Part or the Whole, by way of Reparation, not to mention its being an actual Encouragement to transgress, this Recompence would only be a Means to promote a Multitude of false Accusations; for what Man could live with so much Circumspection, that a Woman might not often have an Opportunity to accuse him of such a Fact, with very probable Circumstances, when there is no Opportunity of detecting the Fallacy. This Difficulty, indeed, is not to be got over; and the Objection lies equally strong against all sorts of Corporal Punishment, Death itself not excepted. For if there are so many false Indictments for *Rapes*, where a Woman receives no Benefit by the Prosecution, where she is liable to such cross Examinations, and where the Possibility of the Fact is so much doubted, that a Woman is generally discountenanc'd, and must bring a Number of probable concurrent Circumstances before she can gain Credit: I say, if notwithstanding these Discouragements, there are so many malicious Prosecutions for *Rapes*, that the Benefit of the Law in general is much disputed, what may we expect in the present Case, where a Woman has nothing to do but acknowledge that she was over-persuaded, and then all Difficulties vanish? Besides, if such a Law was made, setting aside that the Remedy would be worse than the Disease, it is much to be question'd if it prov'd any Remedy at all: For what Fine can we propose as sufficient to deter Men, when there are so many that squander away their whole Fortunes upon this sole Gratification? And what Corporal Punishment, on this side Death, can we find out equivalent to a *Pox*, which they every day run the Risque of?

But no such Law, as yet, has been so much as propos'd, altho' Whoring has been a very obvious Mischief ever since Laws were in Being; therefore, without farther Argument, considering the Wisdom of our *Legislature*, that such a Law never has been made, ought to be sufficient Reason for us to judge it impracticable.

Since the Torrent of Lewdness, then, is too strong to be opposed by open Force, let us see if we can find out an Expedient to divert it by Policy, and prevent the Mischief tho' we can't prevent the Crime.

Most *Authors*, who have writ of Government, have chose to express their Sentiments by comparing the Public Body with the Body Natural; and Mr. *Hobbes*, in his *Leviathan*, has carry'd the *Allegory* as far as it will go. To make Use of it in the present Instance, we may look upon *Whoring* as a Kind of Peccant Humour in the Body-Politic, which, in order to its Discharge, naturally seizes upon such external Members as are most liable to Infection, and at the same time most proper to carry off the Malignity. If this Discharge is promoted by a Licence for *Publick Stews*, which is a Kind of legal Evacuative, the Constitution will certainly be preserv'd: Whereas, if we apply Penal Laws, like violent Astringents, they will only drive the Disease back into the Blood; where, gathering Strength, and at last assimilating the whole Mass, it will break out with the utmost Virulence, to the apparent Hazard of those sound Members, which otherwise might have escaped the Contagion. As we may observe in a *Clap*, where Nature of her own Accord expels the noxious Humour thro' the same Passages by which it was at first receiv'd; but if we resist Nature in this Discharge, and repel the Venom by too hasty an Application of *Styptics*, the Disease then turns to a *Pox*, seizes the Vitals, and, to use *Solomon*'s Words, *like a Dart, strikes thro' the Liver*. But, leaving *Allegory* as more proper for *Rhetoric* or *Poetry*, than such serious Debates, since this Project of the *Public Stews* is the only Expedient now left for the Preservation of Female Chastity, the Question is, Whether or no this Expedient will really answer the End propos'd?

To prove the Affirmative, requires no more but that we look into ourselves, and examine our own Passions; for Love ever was and will be the same in all Men, and in all Ages. The first amorous Emotions that young Men feel, are violent; they are plagued with a Stimulation, which raises a vehement Desire: The Passion is strong, but then it is general; it is Lust, not Love: And therefore the natural Impatience of *Lust* will prompt them to take the speediest way for present Gratification, and make them prefer the ready and willing Embraces of a Courtezan, before the doubtful and distant Prospect of enjoying a modest Damsel, whose Coyness will cost so much Pains, as well as Time, to overcome; and, when overcome, may probably occasion a future Uneasiness, and give them more Trouble after Enjoyment than they had before.

Besides this, if their first Affections should happen to be engaged to a particular Object, which is very rare; and that this particular Object was in their Power to compass, which is still rarer; yet there is naturally in Young-Men a certain secret Shame, which attends their first Sallies, and prevents their declaring a private Passion, 'till it grows so violent, that they are forced to give it Vent upon the Publick; and by that means, get into a regular Method of making themselves easy, without doing their Modesty any Violence.

But tho' the natural Bent of Men's Minds inclines them to an easy Purchase of Pleasure in their first Amours, yet publick Whoring lies at present under so many Disadvantages; the Publick Women, for want of good Regulation, are so infamous in their Principles and Practice; the Places of Resort so vile, and so scandalously imposing in the common Expence, and lying under the Lash of the *Civil* Power, so pester'd with the mercenary Officiousness of *Reforming Constables*; and which is worst of all, the Plague of *Claps* and *Poxes* is so inevitable, that Men contrary to their Inclinations are often forc'd to enter upon private Intrigues, either without trying the Publick, or after meeting with some Misfortunes in the Tryal.

Now if we see daily so many Young Men, who prefer the publick Commerce under all these Disadvantages, what Success may we not expect from this happy Establishment of the *Stews*, when the Young Women's Behaviour will be regulated after a civil decent Manner; when the Houses of Entertainment will be so Commodious, and the Expence of Accomodation so reasonable; when the horrid Dread of *Claps* is entirely remov'd; and when the Laws, instead of disturbing such Assemblies, will be employ'd in their Protection, to give them the greater Countenance and Encouragement; surely we may hope for a thorough Reformation.

But if these Considerations should not prove fully effectual, and some Men should be so obstinate as to persist in private Whoring, notwithstanding these Inducements to the contrary; we must then have Recourse to *Legal* Force, and drive those who are too resty to be led: For tho' the Laws can't prevent Whoring, they may yet regulate it; the *Quid* is not in their Power, but the *Quomodo* is. A Man must eat, but he may be directed how to eat. The strongest Curb can't stop an unruly Horse, but the weakest will serve to turn him: And the smallest Stream is not to be obstructed, tho' we can change the Course of the greatest River. So Love, tho' ever so unruly and headstrong in the general, changes the particular Object of its Passion with the smallest Circumstance; and legal Penalties are no trifling Dissuasives, when the Laws don't command Impossibilities.

This Argument indeed, of Compulsion, is in a manner supernumerary, and thrown in, as it were, *ex abundanti*: For *the Publick Stews* under this regular Oeconomy, will have so much the Advantage of private Whoring, whether we regard the Ease and Conveniency of Enjoyment, or the Beauty and Variety of Mistresses, that Men's natural Inclinations will sway them sufficiently without this superfluous Constraint. If there is any Fear of Success, the Danger lies on the other Side; and indeed we have some Colour of Reason to apprehend, lest the whole Body of Lewdness being turn'd upon the Publick, there should want a sufficient Supply of young Women to recruit the *Stews*; which, by that Means, may run into a sudden Dis-repute, and lose a Character that will be difficult to retrieve. But however plausible this Objection may seem at first Sight, we shall find, upon a nearer View, that it only serves to make the Excellence of this Scheme the more manifest.

As there is constantly in the Nation, a certain Number of young Men, whose Passions are too strong to brook any Opposition: Our Business is to contrive a Method how they may be gratify'd, with as little Expence of Female Virtue as possible. But the Difficulty lies in adjusting this Matter, and gaging our young Men's Affections so exactly, that the Modesty of one Woman may not be sacrifis'd, more than is absolutely necessary for the Preservation of the rest.

The Gallants of this Age, indeed, are not quite so sturdy as that rampant *Roman* Emperor who deflower'd ten *Sarmatian* Virgins in one Night; but what we want in Constitution, we make up in the Niceity of our Palates; as a squeamish Stomach requires the greatest Variety of Dishes: And some of our Youth are grown such perfect *Epicures* in Venery, that they can relish nothing but *Virgins*: They destroy, it is true, a great deal of Beauty, by browsing only upon the Buds.

But we ought not to judge of these Men's Abilities by the Number of Women they debauch, no more than we should measure the Goodness of a certain curious Gentleman's Appetite by his bespeaking several Dozen of young Pigeons, when he only regal'd upon the Rumps: Neither is it intirely from a Wantonness of Fancy, or a luxurious Taste of Pleasure, that Men indulge themselves in making this Havock, but chiefly for their own personal Safety. Young Girls are so giddy, thoughtless, and unexperienc'd, and withal so fond of the Sport, at their first setting out, that they seldom escape a Taint; and a Man is not safe in being constant: Nay, some Men are afraid of venturing even after themselves. By this Means several likely Women, that might do the Publick signal Service, are in a short Time render'd useless: And, by a modest Computation, we are put to the Expence of as many virtuous Women in one Year, as might reasonably serve the Nation six.

Now, the *Publick Stews* will regulate this Affair so precisely, and with such critical Exactness, that one Year with another, we shall not have one Woman employ'd in the Publick Service more than is absolutely necessary, nor one less than is fully sufficient.

When this Project is first set on foot, the vast Choice and Variety there is at present of these Women, will give us an Opportunity of making a very beautiful Collection; and will, doubtless, for some Time, occasion a considerable Run upon the Publick; so that *Private Whoring*, the only Nursery of our Courtezans, may probably remain too long neglected: For the whole Body of our incontinent Youth, like a standing Army, being employ'd in constant Action, there cannot well be spar'd a sufficient Detachment to raise the necessary Recruits.

But however true this may be, we shall thereby suffer no Inconvenience; for if the Supplies of young Women, which we may reasonably expect from the Northern and Western Parts of these Kingdoms, or from such Places as are remote and out of the Influence of this *Scheme*: I say, if these Supplies should not prove sufficient to answer the Greatness of the Demand, and that the Reputation of the *Stews* upon this Account, should begin to flag, why then the worst Accident that can befal, is a gradual Relapse into our former State of *Private Whoring*; and this no farther than is just necessary and to recruit the *Stews*, and thereby make them retrieve their former Character: For every Woman who is debauch'd more than is barely necessary, only brings so much additional Credit and Reputation to the *Stews*, and in some measure atones for the Loss of her own Chastity, by being a Means to preserve that of others; so that whenever the Tide of private Lewdness runs too high, and exceeds the just and ordinary Bounds, it must of Course, by encouraging the *Publick Stews*, immediately suffer a proportionable Ebb: That is to say, it must be reduced again so low, that there will remain but just a sufficient Quantity to supply the *Stews*; which is as low, as in the Nature of the Thing is possible.

I might here lavish out Encomiums, and take Occasion to dwell upon those many Advantages that will accrue to the *Nation* by this admirable Scheme; but shall only take Notice of this peculiar Excellence, which it has above all other Schemes, that it necessarily executes itself.

But since the Necessity of debauching a certain Number of young Women, is entirely owing to the Necessity of supplying the *Public Stews*; a Question may very reasonably arise, whether this Project might not be vastly improv'd, even to the total Extirpation of *Private Whoring*, by an Act *for encouraging the Importation of foreign Women*. This, I must confess, deserves a serious Debate: for, besides the Honour of our Females, which would be preserv'd by such an Act, it might bring this farther Advantage; That whereas most of our estated Youth spend a great Part of their Time and Fortunes in travelling Abroad, for no other End, as it seems by most of them, but to be inform'd in the *French* and *Italian* Gallantry; they would then have an Opportunity of satisfying their Curiosity in Foreign Amours, without stirring out of *London*. But I shall leave the Decision of this Matter to abler Pens, well knowing, that a Truth of this Nature, which carries so much the Air of Novelty, will require much better Authority than mine to warrant it.

Let it suffice for the present, that I have fully prov'd what I at first propos'd in this Treatise: That *Public Whoring* is neither so criminal in itself, nor so detrimental to the *Society*, as *Private Whoring*; and that the encouraging of *Publick Whoring*, by erecting *Stews* for that Purpose, will not only prevent most of the mischievous Consequences of this Vice, but even lessen the Quantity of *Whoring* in general, and reduce it to the narrowest Bounds which it can possibly be contain'd in.

After what has been said, it may, perhaps, appear somewhat odd to talk of Religious Objections, as if either Christianity or Morality could possibly object against a *Scheme*, which is entirely calculated for the Welfare and Happiness of Mankind. But since a great many Men amongst us have entertained such whimsical Notions of Religion, as to imagine, that in some Cases, a Law may be unjust and wicked, tho' it evidently promotes the Publick Good: as if the right Enjoyment of this Life was inconsistent with our Happiness in the next: I say, since many Men of Understanding have suffer'd themselves to be possess'd with this mistaken Principle, I shall, as briefly as may be, answer such Objections as can, with any Colour of Reason, be offer'd.

First then, I expect to be attack'd with that old moral Precept, of *Not doing Evil that Good may come of it*. This may be answer'd with another old Saying, equally authentic, and more applicable to the present Purpose, that *of two Evils we ought to chuse the least*. The Case is this: A private Member of a *Society*, may, doubtless, commit a Crime with a Design to promote the Good of that *Society*, which was partly the Case of *Felton* against the Duke of *Buckingham*; and this evil Action may possibly answer the Goodness of the

Intention, but is universally condemn'd as an unwarrantable Presumption; and falls justly under the Censure of doing a certain Evil, for the Prospect of an uncertain Good. But as to the *Legislature*, there is a wide Difference; for they, and they only, are intrusted with the Welfare of the *Society*: This Publick Welfare is, or ought to be, the whole End and Scope of their Actions; and they are fully impower'd to do whatever they judge conducive to that End. If their Intentions come up to this, they are certainly in their Consciences acquitted: But as to the World, their Actions, that is, their Laws, are judg'd good or bad, just or unjust, according as they actually prove beneficial or detrimental to the *Society* in general: And therefore it is the grossest Absurdity, and a perfect Contradiction in Terms, to assert, That a *Government* may not commit Evil that Good may come of it; for, if a Publick Act, taking in all its Consequences, really produces a greater Quantity of Good, it must, and ought to be term'd a good Act; altho' the bare Act, consider'd in itself, without the consequent Good, should be in the highest Degree wicked and unjust.

As for Instance: A Ship performing Quarantine, and known to be infected, is sunk by a Storm; some of the Crew, half drown'd, recover the Shore; but the Moment they land, the *Government* orders them to be shot to Death. This Action, in itself, is no less than a downright unchristian and inhuman Murther; but since the Health and Safety of the Nation is secured by this severe Precaution, it is no Wonder, if we allow the Action to be not only justifiable, but in the strictest Sense of Morality Just.

Another Objection, or rather the same set in a stronger Light, is, That altho' the Welfare and Happiness of the Community is, or ought to be, the only End of all Law and Government, yet since our spiritual Welfare is the *Summum Bonum* which all Christians should aim at, no Christian Government ought to authorize the Commission of the least known Sin, tho' for the greatest temporal Advantage.

To this Objection, I answer, That it is universally allow'd as one of the greatest Perfections of the Christian Religion, that its Precepts are calculated to promote the Happiness of Mankind in this World as well as the next; if so, then it is a direct Arraignment of the Lawgiver's infinite Wisdom, *i. e.* a Contradiction to assert, that, in Matters of Law and Government, the Publick Breach of any Gospel Precept can possibly be for the temporal Good of any *Society* whatever: And therefore we may with Confidence affirm, that no sinful Laws can be beneficial, and *vice versa*, that no beneficial Laws can be sinful. Now we have already given sufficient Proof of the Benefit the *Public* would receive by licensing the *Stews*, and therefore ought to conclude such Licence lawful; but lest the apparent Wickedness of the *Stews*, should be objected against this general Reasoning, it is fit that we examine this Matter a little nearer.

Fornication is, no doubt, a direct Breach of a *Gospel*-Precept, and is therefore a Sin; but this Sin, barely as such, concerns the *Government* no more than the Eating of *Black-puddings*, equally prohibited in the same 8 Text. The Reason is this: The Sin consists in a full Intention to gratify a Lustful Desire; which Intention the *Legislature* cannot possibly prevent: Penalties indeed may deter Men from gratifying their Desires, at the Expence of the Public, but will rather increase than lessen the Desires themselves. If it is argu'd, that the Sin of the Intention is aggravated by being put in Execution, so much the better for our Purpose; for then the Argument stands thus:

Since the Sin of the Intention is entirely out of the *Legislature*'s Power, the utmost they can do, with regard to this Sin, is, to prevent its being aggravated by actual Commission.

But the *Public Stews*, as we have already prov'd, will prevent as much as possible this actual Commission.

Therefore the *Publick Stews* will prevent as much as possible this SIN.

Another Branch of this Objection, without which the Objection itself would be of no Force, is, that the authorizing of *Public Stews* is a Public Encouragement for People to Whore.

If by People are meant those in the *Stews*, I hope it will be thought no Crime to encourage such People, rather to confine themselves to the Practice of one Vice, than live by committing a Thousand; especially when that one Vice is what they would really practise, whether they were encourag'd or not.

But if any imagine that this particular Licence would be a general Encouragement to the whole *Nation*, they are certainly mistaken. For, as to the Men, they are already as bad as they can be; if any Thing cures them, it must be *Satiety*: Let them have full and free Leave to take a Surfeit of unlawful Love, and they will soon learn to prefer the Chaste Embraces of Innocence before the bought Smile of Harlots loveless, joyless, unindear'd casual Fruition.

It is a right Observation, that Restraint does but whet a Man's Passions instead of curing them.

Exuperat magis, ægrescitque medendo. Æn. 12. And a late ingenious *Author*, who study'd Mankind, speaking on this Subject, has these Words: *To put down* Publick Stews, *is not only to disperse Fornication into all Parts, but, by the Difficulty, to excite wild and wanton People to this Vice.*

It was observ'd at *Rome*, that in the full Liberty of Divorces, there was not a single Instance of one in fifty Years: And that *Cato* long'd for his Wife again as soon as she was in another's Possession.

The Master of Love says positively,

Quod licet ingratum est, quod non licet acrius urit.

And *Martial* speaking to a married Rake, *B*. 3. *Ep*. 68. says,

Cur aliena placet tibi, quæ tua non placet uxor? Nunquid Securus non potes arrigere?

I pr'ythee tell me why a Wife
   Thy am'rous Fancy never warms?
What! without Danger o'thy Life,
   Cannot thy Cod-pice stand to Arms?

     And again, *B*. 1. *Ep*. 74.

Nullus in urbe fuit tota, qui tangere vellet
Uxorem gratis, Cæciliane, tuam
Dum licuit: sed nunc, positis custodibus, ingens
Turba fututorum est. Ingeniosus Homo es.

There's no Man, *Cæcil*, in the Town,
   Would, *gratis*, have enjoy'd thy Spouse;
But how thou art so jealous grown,
   Lord! what a Croud about the House!
You've lock'd her up, t'increase her Value;
In short, you are a cunning Fellow.

The *Public Stews* will not encourage Men to be lewd, but they will encourage them to exercise their Lewdness in a proper Place, without disturbing the Peace of the *Society*, and with as little Detriment to themselves as possible. And, as to the Women, there's not the least Shadow of Encouragement: For no modest Woman ever lost her Maiden-head with the dismal Prospect of becoming a *Public Courtezan*: And if a Woman is not modest, the licensing of the *Public Stews* is no more an Encouragement for her to practise, than the allowing a certain Number of Hackney-Coaches every *Sunday* is an Encouragement for the rest to ply; when the very Licence, to some, expresly implies a Prohibition of the rest.

Having now sufficiently proved the Institution of the *Public Stews* to be a Political Good, and answer'd all the religious Objections against it; I shall conclude with observing, That I have the Authority of *Italy*, the most Politic Nation in the World, to back me in the first Part of my Argument; and the Opinion of *Holland*, one of the strictest Reformed Churches, to vindicate me in the second; and that we ourselves enjoy'd the Benefit of this Institution till we were depriv'd of it by the over-hasty Zeal of our first Reformers in the sixteenth Century.

The *Public Stews* were antiently kept in *Southwark*, by an express Licence from the Government, and open Permission both Civil and Ecclesiastical, for they paid regular Taxes to the *Lord-Mayor* of the *City*, and to the Bishop of the *See*.

We do not find that they were ever molested 'till the 25th of *Edward* the Third, when, in the Parliament at *Westminster*, at the Request of the *Londoners*, says *Daniel*, an Act passed, obliging all Common Whores to distinguish themselves, by wearing Hoods striped with divers Colours, or Furs, and their Gowns turn'd *inside* out.

This, indeed, was but a Trifle to what they suffer'd thirty Years after by *Wat Tyler*'s Rebellion.

In the fifth of *Richard* the Second, *Wat* marched up from *Dartworth*, with a true Spirit of Reformation, fully resolv'd to burn and destroy every thing that oppos'd him: If the Archbishop's Palace at *Lambeth* could not escape, there was little Mercy to be expected for the *Stews* 9; besides, Whoring was not the least of *Wat*'s Grievances: He began his Rebellion by killing a Collector of the Poll-Tax for being a little too brisk upon his Daughter; and his Antipathy to the *Stews* was still increased, by the *Lord-Mayor*'s shutting the City-Gates, and denying him Entrance; for he could not revenge the Affront more effectually, than by *cutting off so large a Branch of his Lordship's Revenue*.

In short, every thing concurred to the Destruction of the *Stews*, and demolish'd they were.

This Action, however, lost *Tyler* his Life; for *William Walworth*, then Lord-Mayor, was the very Man who struck him first off his Horse in *Smithfield*: For which the King knighted him, gave him 100 *l*. Pension, and added the Dagger to the City-Arms.

Whilst Whoring was in this unsettled Condition, the *Bishop* thought it a good Opportunity to ingross the whole Profit of licensing Courtezans, which occasion'd them fresh Trouble; for *John Northampton*, who succeeded *Walworth*, either piqued at the Bishop's invading his Right, or out of a real Reforming Principle, for he was a Follower of *Wickliff*, commenced a severe Persecution. He had his Spies and Constables in every Street, to apprehend Strollers; and such Women as were neither handsome nor rich enough to bribe his Officers, were carried through the Streets in great Pomp, with their Hair shorn, and Trumpets and Pipes playing before them. All this he did contrary to the express Commands of the Bishop, who had several Bickerings with him upon that Head.

This great Reformer *John Northampton* was, from his troublesome Temper, nick-nam'd *Cumber-Town*; and as he succeeded *Tyler* in the Work of Reformation, so he had like to have met with as bad a Fate: For two Years after he was found guilty of High Treason, without making the least Defence; had his Goods confiscated, and was condemned to perpetual Imprisonment 100 Miles from *London*: Accordingly he was sent to *Tentagil-Castle* in *Cornwall*.

This dreadful *Cumber-Town* being removed, the *Stews* had Leisure to re-settle themselves under the Protection of the Church; and enjoyed an almost uninterrupted Tranquillity for 150 Years.

We find, indeed, an Act passed at *Westminster*, in the 11th of *Hen.* VI. that no Keepers of *Stews*, or *Whore-Houses* in *Southwark*, should be impannelled upon any Jury, or keep a Tavern in any other Place.

But the most sensible Blow they ever felt, was the Invasion of the *French-Pox*. The *Spaniards* had brought it from the Islands of *Florida* to *Naples*, and the Army of *Charles* VIII. when he conquer'd that Kingdom in the Year 1495, transmitted it into *France*, from whence it had a very quick Passage into *England*; for there was an Act passed in the latter end of *Henry* VII's Reign, for expelling out of the *Stews* all such Women as had the Faculty of *Burning*

Men.

However, we find they still continued in good Repute in the Reign of *Henry* VIII.<u>10</u> and yielded a considerable Revenue to the *Bishop* of *London*; for *Bucer*, in one of his Books against *Gardiner*, taxes him with it as *an heinous Crime, that he should receive most of his Rents out of the Public Stews.*

After this terrible Accusation, we may easily guess what Quarter our *Stews* met with at the Reformation. But now *Bucer* has got his Ends; the *Stews* are destroy'd; those public Nusances are demolish'd; Whoring is attack'd on all hands without Mercy; and what then? Why, truly, by mere Dint of *Reforming*, we have reduced Lewdness to that pass, that hardly one Bachelor in the Kingdom will lie with a Woman, if he is sure that she's not found; and very few modest Women will suffer a Man to get them with Child, unless he makes a Promise to marry.

In short, the Truth is, we are at this present Writing as *bad* as we can be; and I hope I have fairly shown how we may be *better*.

APPENDIX.

NUMBER I.

*R*ICHARD RAWLINSON, L. L. D. and R. S. S. in his Account of *Southwark*, <u>11</u> informs us, that next to the *Bear-Garden* on the Bank-Side was formerly the Bo r d e l l o , or St e w e s , so called from several Licensed Houses for the Entertainment of Lewd Persons, in which were Women prepared for all Comers. They were subject to several Laws and Regulations, and their Manner of Life and Privileged Places, received several Confirmations from the Crown.

In 1162, King *Henry* II, in a *Parliament* held at *Westminster*, passed an Act, confirming several Ordinances, Statutes, and old Customs observed in that Place, amongst which the following are remarkable:

That no *Stew-Holder* or his Wife, should lett or stay any single Woman to go and come freely at all Times when she listed.

No *Stewholder* to keep any Woman to board, but she to board abroad at her Pleasure.

To take no more for the Woman's Chamber than *fourteen* Pence.

Not to keep open his Doors upon the Holy-days.

Not to keep any single Woman in his House on the Holy-days, but the *Bailiff* to see them voided out of the Lordship.

No single Woman to be kept against her Will, that would leave her Sin.

No *Stew-Holder* to receive any Woman of Religion, or any Mans Wife.

No single Woman to take Money to lie with any Man, except she lye with him all Night, till the Morrow.

No Man to be drawn or enticed into any *Stew-House*.

The *Constables*, *Bailiffs*, and others, were every Week to search every *Stew-House*.

No *Stew-Holder* to keep any Woman that hath the perillous Infirmity of *Burning*, nor to sell Bread, Ale, Flesh, Fish, Wood, Coal, or any sort of Victuals.

Anno 1345, Stews were licenced by King *Edward* III. Anno 1381, these Stew-Houses belonged to *William Walworth*, Lord-Mayor of *London*, who let them out to some *Flemish* Women, and soon after they were plundered by *Walter Tyler*, and the rebellious *Kentishmen*, when probably they were put down, and again suffered, and afterwards confirmed by *Henry* VI. In 1506, King *Henry* VII. for some Time shut up these Houses, which were in Number *Eighteen*, and not long after renewed their Licence, and reduced them to *Twelve*; at which Number they continued till their final Suppression by Sound of Trumpet, in 1546, by King *Henry* VIII, whose tender Conscience startled at such scandalous and open Lewdness. The single Women who were Retainers to, or Inmates in, these Houses, were excommunicated, not suffered to enter the Church while alive, or if not reconciled before their Death, prohibited Christian Burial, and were interred in a Piece of Ground called the *Single-Women's Church-Yard*, set a-part for their Use only. These Houses were distinguished by several Signs painted on their Fronts, as, a *Boar's-Head*, the *Crane*, the *Cardinal's Hat*, the *Swan*, the *Bell*, the *Castle*, the *Cross-Keys*, and the *Gun*.

NUMBER II.

An Attempt to prove the Antiquity of the Venereal Disease, *long before the Discovery of the* West-Indies; *in a Letter to Dr.* JAMES DOUGLASS, *M. D.*

S I R ,

THE Undertaking I am at present engaged in, is to prove that the *Venereal Disease* was known among us, much earlier than the *Æra*, which has been generally assign'd for its Rise by modern Authors; for it is believed it was not known, at least in *Europe*, till about the Year 1494. Notwithstanding which, I determine to make it evident, that it was frequent among us some Hundreds of Years before that Date. I could mention several Physicians and Surgeons of Eminence, who have been of the same Sentiments, particularly, the Learned Dr. *Charles Patin*, who has written a curious Dissertation to prove the *Antiquity of this Disease*, which is sufficient to excuse me from the Imputation of having started a Novelty, or being at the trouble of quoting antient Authorities before taken notice of, from the most ancient Writers of Medicine; as *Hippocrates, Galen, Avicen, Celsus*, &c. and even the *Holy Scriptures*. I shall therefore lay aside all those foreign Aids and Assistances, and trace out the Symptoms of the Disease, as they naturally arise, from the *first* Infection to the *last* destructive Period, and shew that, by searching into our own Antiquities, we may be furnished with Instances of the Frequency of the Distemper among us, in all its respective Stages, before ever our Modern Authors dream it had its Appearance in *Europe*,

I shall begin with the *first* Degree of this Disease, and prove from authentic Evidences, it was anciently call'd the *Brenning* or *Burning*; and that this Word has been successively continu'd for many Hundreds of Years, to signify the same Disease we now call a *Clap*; and that it was not discontinu'd till that Appellation first began to have its Rise. The most likely Method to accomplish my Design, will be first to examine those Records that relate to the *Stews*, which were by Authority allowed to be kept on the *Bank-Side* in *Southwark*, under the Jurisdiction of the Bp. of *Winchester*, and which were suppressed the *37th* of *Hen.* VIII. For it is impossible but, if there were any such Distemper in being at that Time, it must be pretty common among those lewd Women who had a Licence for entertaining their Paramours, notwithstanding any Rules or Orders which might be establish'd to prevent its Increase: But if we shall find that there were Orders establish'd to prevent the Spreading of such a Disease, that Persons might be secure from any contagious Malady after their Entertainment at those Houses (which were anciently 18 in Number, but in the Reign of *Hen.* VII. reduced to 12) we may then securely depend upon it, that it was the Frequency of the Disease that put those who had the Authority, under a necessity of making such Rules and Orders. For the same Powers, who granted a Liberty for keeping open such lewd Houses, must find it their Interest to secure, as much as possible, all Persons from receiving any Injury there; lest the Frequency of such Misfortunes should deter others from frequenting them, and so the original Design of their Institution cease; from the entire sinking of the Revenues. Now I find that, as early as the Year 1162, divers Constitutions relating to the Lordship of *Winchester*, (being also confirmed by the King) were to be kept for ever, according to the old Customs that had been Time out of Mind. Among which these were some, *viz.* 1. *No Stew-holder to take more for a Woman's Chamber in the Week than 14 d.* 2. *Not to keep open his Doors upon Holy Days.* 3. *No single Woman to be kept against her Will, that would leave her Sin.* 4. *No single Woman to take Money to be with any Man, except she lie with him all Night till the Morning.* 5. *No Stew-holder to keep any Woman that hath the perilous Infirmity of Burning.* These and many more Orders were to be strictly observed, or the Offenders to be severely punished. Now we are assured, there is no other Disease that can be communicated by *Carnal-Conversation* with Women, but that which is *Venereal*, by reason that only is contagious; and its evident the *Burning* was certainly so: For, had it been nothing else but some simple Ulceration, Heat, or Inflammation, there would have been no Contagion; and that affecting only the Woman, could not be communicated by any *Venereal Congress*, and so not infer a Necessity of her being comprehended under the restraining Article. These Orders likewise prove the Disease was much more ancient than the Date above-mentioned; because they were only a Renewal of such as had been before established Time out of Mind.

But to confirm this farther, I find that in the Custody of the Bp. of *Winchester*, whose Palace was situate on the *Bank-side*, near the *Stews*, was a Book written upon Vellum, the Title of which runs thus: *Here begynne the*

Ordinances, Rules, and Customs, as well for the Salvation of Mannes Life, as for to aschew many Mischiefs and Inconvenients that daily be lik there for to fall out, to be rightfully kept, and due Execution of them to be done unto any Person within the same. One of the Articles begins thus: *De his qui custodiunt Mulieres habentes Nephandam infirmitatem.* It goes on, *Item, That no Stewholder keep noo Woman wythin his House, that hath any Sickness of* BRENNING, *but that she be put out upon the peyne of makeit a fine unto the Lord of a hundred Shillings.* This is taken from the Original Manuscript, which was preserv'd in the Bishop's Court, suppos'd to be written about the Year 1430. From these Orders we may observe the Frequency of the Distemper at that Time; which, with other Inconveniences, was *dayly like there for to fall out*: and the Greatness of the Penalty, as the Value of Money then was, that is laid on it, proves it was no trifling or insignificant thing.

But the bare Proof of there having been anciently such a Disease as was called the *Burning*, may be thought to be insufficient, unless we were perfectly assured what it was, and how it was in those Times described: I shall therefore do it from an unquestionable Authority, which is that of *John Arden,* Esq; who was one of the Surgeons to King *Richard* II. and likewise to King *Henry* IV. In a curious Manuscript of his upon Vellum, he defines it to be, a certain inward Heat and Excoriation of the *Urethra*; which Description gives us a perfect Idea of what we now call a *Clap*; for frequent Dissections of those who laboured under that Disease, have made it evident, that their *Urethra* is excoriated by the Virulency of the Matter they receive from the infected Woman; and this Excoriation or Ulceration is not confined to the *Ostiola* or Mouths of the *Glandulæ Muscosæ* as has been lately thought, but may equally alike attack any Part of the *Urethra* not beyond the reach of the impelled malignant Matter. The Heat before described, which these Persons are sensible of, as well now as formerly, is a Consequent of the excoriated *Urethra*; for the Salts contained in the Urine must necessarily prick and irritate the nervous *Fibrillæ*, and excite a Heat in those Parts of the *Urethra* which are divested of its natural Membrane; which Heat will always be observed to be more or less, as the Salts are diluted with a greater or less Quantity of Urine; a thing I have often observed in Persons who have laboured under this Infirmity in hot Weather, when the perspirable Matter being thrown off in greater Quantities, the Salts bear a greater Proportion to the Quantity of Urine, and thereby make its Discharge at that Time so much the more painful and troublesome.

Thus we see this very early and plain Description of this Disease among us, to be entirely conformable to the latest and most exact Anatomical Discoveries. Here is no Tone of the *Testicles* depraved, according to *Trajanus Petronius*; no Exulceration of the *Parastatæ*, according to *Rondeletius*; no Ulceration of the *Seminal Vessels*, according to *Platerus*; no Seat of the Disease in the *Vesiculæ Seminales*, or *Prostatæ*, according to *Bartholin*; nor in those Parts and the Testicles at the same Time, according to our Countryman *Wharton* and others, who have falsly fixed the Seat of this Disease, and whose Notions, in this respect, are now justly exploded; but a single and true Description of it, and its Situation, about 150 Years before any of those Gentlemen obliged the World with their learned Labours.

Having, I hope, sufficiently made it appear, the *Burning* was a Disease very early among us, and given the Description of it, I shall proceed to say something of the ancient Method that was made use of to cure it. We are not to expect the Measures our Predecessors, in those early Times, made use of, should be calculated for the removing any Malignity in the Mass of Blood, or other Juices, according to the Practice in Venereal Cases at this Time; because they looked upon the Disease to be entirely local, and the Whole of the Cure to depend upon the Removal of the Symptoms: Hence it was they recommended such Remedies as were accommodated to the taking off the inward Heat of the Part, and cure the Excoriations or Ulcerations of the *Urethra*. The Process for the accomplishing of this, I shall set down from the before-mentioned *John Arden*, who wrote about the Year 1380, His Words are as follow: *Contra Incendium. Item contra Incendium Virgæ Virilis interius ex calore & excoriatione, fiat talis Syringa* (i. e. *Injectio*) *lenitiva. Accipe Lac mulieris masculum nutrientis, & parum zucarium, Oleum violæ & ptisanæ, quibus commixtis per Syringam infundator, & si prædictis admiscueris lac Amigdalarum melior erit medicina.* There is no doubt but this Remedy, being used to our Patients at this Time, would infallibly take off the inward Heat of the Part, and cure the Excoriations or Ulcerations of the *Urethra*, by which means what issued from thence would be entirely stopt: and this was all they expected from their Medicines, forasmuch as they were entirely unacquainted with the Nature of the Distemper; and did not in the least imagine, but if the Symptoms that first attack'd the Part were removed, the Patient was entirely cured.

I shall now, as a farther Confirmation of what I have advanced, proceed to prove, that by this *Brenning* or *Burning* is meant the *Venereal Disease*, by demonstrating that succeeding Historians, Physical and Chirurgical Writers, and others, have all along with us in *England* used the very same Word to signify the Venereal Malady. In an old Manuscript, I have, written about the Year 1390. is a Receipt for *Brenning of the Pyntyl, yat Men clepe ye Apegalle*; *Galle* being an old English Word for a running Sore. They who know the *Etymology* of the Word *Apron*, cannot be ignorant of this. And in another Manuscript, written about 50 Years after, is a Receipt for *Burning* in that Part by a Woman. *Simon Fish*, a zealous Promoter of the *Reformation* in the Reign of *Hen.* VIII. in his Supplication of Beggars, presented to the King, in 1530, says as follows, *These be they* (speaking of the *Romish Priests*) *that corrupt the whole Generation of Mankind in your Realm, that catch the Pockes of one Woman and bear them to another; that be* Burnt *with one Woman and bear it to another; that catch the Lepry of one Woman and bare it unto another.* But to make this Matter still more evident, I am to observe, that *Andrew Boord, M. D.* and Romish Priest, in the same Reign, in a Book he wrote, entitl'd *The Breviary of Health*, printed in 1546, speaks very particularly of this sort of *Burning*; one of his Chapters beginneth thus, *The 19th Chapiter doth shew of* BURNING *of an Harlot*; where his Notion of communicating the *Burning* is very particular. He adds, that if a Man be *Burnt* with an *Harlot*, and do meddle with another Woman within a Day, he shall *Burn* her; and as an immediate Remedy against the *Burning*, he recommends the washing the *Pudenda* 2 or 3 times with White Wine, or else with Sack and Water; but if the Matter have continued long, to go to an expert Surgeon for Help. In his 82d *Chapter*, he speaks of *two* sorts of *Burning*, the *One* by *Fire*, and the *Other* by a *Woman* thro' carnal Copulation, and refers the Person that is *Burnt* of a *Harlot* to another Chapter of his for Advice, what to do, *yf he get a Dorser or two*, so called from its Protuberancy or bunching out: For I find about that Time the Word *Bubo* was mostly made use of, to signify that sort of Swelling which usually happens in pestilential Diseases.

From hence it appears, the *Burning*, by its Consequents, was *Venereal*; since every Day's Experience makes it evident, that the ill Treatment of the first Symptoms of the Disease, either by astringent Medicines, or the removing them by cooling and healing the excoriated Parts, will generally be attended with such Swellings in the Groin, which we rarely observe to happen from any other Cause whatsoever.

I shall give a few more Instances of this Disease being call'd the *Burning*, and conclude. In a Manuscript I have of the Vocation of *John Bale* to the Bishoprick of *Ossory* in *Ireland*, written by himself, he speaks of Dr. *Hugh Weston* (who was Dean of *Windsor* in 1556. but deprived by Cardinal *Pole* for Adultery) as follows; "At this Day is lecherous *Weston*, who is more practised in the Art of *Brech-Burning* than all the *Whores* of the *Stews*. And again, speaking of the same Person, he says, "He not long ago *brent* a *Beggar* in St. *Botolph*'s Parish. The same Author says of him elsewhere, "He had ben *sore Bitten* with a *Winchester Goose*, and was not yet healed thereof; which was a common Phrase for the Pox at that Time, because the *Stews* were under the Jurisdiction of the Bishop of *Winchester*. *Mich. Wood*, in his *Epistle* before *Stephen Gardiner*'s Oration *de vera Obedientia*, printed at *Rhoan*, 1553. gives another Evidence of the *Burning*. And *William Bullein*, a Physician in the Reign of Queen *Eliz.* in a Book he publish'd, call'd *The Bulwark of Defence, &c.* printed in 1562. bringing in *Sickness* demanding of *Health* what he should do with a Disease call'd the *French Pockes*, *Health* answers, *"He would not that any should fishe for this Disease, or to be bold when he is bitten to thynke thereby to be helped, but rather to eschewe the Cause of thys Infirmity, and filthy rotten Burning of Harlots.*

London, Feb. 4.   W i l l i a m B e c k e t t,
1717–18.

NUMBER III.

A Second Letter on the same Subject to WILLIAM WAGSTAFFE, M. D.

SIR,

B E F O R E I engage farther, in proving that the *Venereal Disease*, when it came to be confirmed, was frequently known among us some hundreds of Years before the Siege of *Naples*: I shall endeavour to refute the Opinion of those Persons, who believe it to have had its Rise there, if any such shall remain. True indeed it is, that there have not been wanting several modern Authors, who have asserted it; but I determine to make it appear to be an Error as inconsiderately, and hastily received, as started by some Chimerical Author; who, because several Writers about that time, observing the Disease to begin in the *Pudenda*, separated it from another, with which it was before confounded, must likewise take upon him to assert its being a *new* Distemper, and to assign a certain Time and Place for its Rise. Now one might with all the Reason in the World expect, that if the Disease had its Original there, it must have been so certainly and infallibly known, that there could have been no doubtful or uncertain Opinions about it, but that the Physicians, who resided *in* or *near* the Place, and those more especially, who interested themselves so far as to write of it, must have, all of them to a Man, agreed upon the Certainty of a thing, the Knowledge of the Truth of which was so easily attainable. But on the contrary, *Nicholas Leonicenus*, who was the first *Italian* Physician, that wrote of this Disease, and who lived at the very time, when *Naples* was besieged, is so far from acknowledging it to have had its Rise there, from the *French* Soldiers Conversation with the *Italian* Women, and so little did he know of its true Cause, that he does not allow it to be the Consequent of impure Embraces. About this time it was likewise, that Pope *Alexander* the VIth engaged *Gaspar Torella* to write of this Distemper. This Pope was in League with *Alphonsus* King of *Naples*, against *Charles* VIII. King of *France*, to prevent his passing thro' *Italy*, when he went to besiege *Naples*; yet this Author is so far from allowing it to have had its Original there, that he tells us, the Astrologers were of opinion, that it proceeded from I know not what particular Constellations. Nor does *Sebastianus Aquilanus*, who lived at that time, allow it to be any other than an ancient Disease; or *Antonius Scanarolius*, who wrote in 1498, which was but 4 or 5 Years after that Siege. Nor do several other Authors, then living, say one Word about this *Neapolitan* Story. But it seems *Ulricus de Hutten*, a *German* Kt. no Physician, positively affirms this Disease to have had its Rise there; but how he should come to know this, who lived at such a distance from the Place, and they, who were Physicians residing as it were upon the Spot, be ignorant of it, will be as much credited, as his following inconsistent Relation, which will sufficiently prove, how little care he took to be apprised of the Truth of what he wrote. This very Author tells us, the Disease was unknown till the Year 1493, or thereabouts; that he himself had it, when he was a Child, and so consequently that it was hereditary, or from the Nurse. He Wrote his Book of this Distemper at *Mentz,* where it was printed by *John Scheffer* in 4*to,* 1519. Now if we allow him to be but 27 Years of Age, when he wrote, (for he cannot be suppos'd to be less, who before this took upon him to cure his Father of the *Venereal Disease,* without the Assistance of any Physician or Surgeon,) he must have had the Distemper upon him, according to his own Account, before ever it was in being. Thus we may see, how Persons may be impos'd upon by a hasty and inconsistent Writer, no way qualified for such an Undertaking, and greedily receive in Falshoods instead of Truths, if they will not be at the Pains of consulting the Original Writings of our Predecessors, the only sure Method of overthrowing such chimerical and imaginary Notions.

I have in my former Letters, to Dr. Do U G L A S S , sufficiently I think proved that the *first* Degree of the *Venereal Disease* was very common among us some hundreds of Years before it is commonly said to have been known in *Europe*; there will be no Reason for any body to conceive we were at that time in any measure Strangers to it, when it came to be confirmed; more especially, when we consider the Methods of Treatment in those Times, which consisting principally in topical Applications, many of their Patients could not possibly escape having it confirmed on them. Now when it was in this confirmed State, the Writers of those early times looked upon it as an *entirely new* Disease, and not a Consequent of any Evil before contracted, because they were not apprised, that the *first* Symptoms being removed, and the Disease to Appearance cured, it should afterwards discover it self in such a manner, as should not seem to have the least Analogy with the Symptoms, that first attack'd a part which had been for a considerable time free from any

Misfortune. But because the Symptoms are the only true Characteristicks, whereby we are infallibly able to know one Disease from another, it may be expected, that I produce sufficient Authorities to demonstrate they were all of them known and described by ancient Physical and Chirurgical Writers, just as they appear to be in the *Venereal Disease* at this Day, if I would prove that *Disease* to be of a much more ancient Date, than is generally thought; and if I do this, I cannot but think it will be satisfactory, since we can have no other way of coming to a Knowledge of any one Distemper, than by its Symptoms. The Method of laying down the exact Succession of them, will be impossible to be reduced to any certain and infallible Rule, there being so great a Variety of Causes, that obstruct such a Regularity; for which Reason, I shall take notice of them in such Order as they most generally appear, which was upon no account to be expected from our antient Writers, insomuch as they mention every particular Symptom by it self, not knowing but that they were independent of each other, and that each of them was a distinct Disease. However, the proving these Symptoms were in being in these *early* times, will be as strong an Argument to prove the Antiquity of this Distemper, as if they had been register'd in the most exact Order of Succession, because we shall, upon the strictest Examination, find they are peculiar to the *Venereal Malady* only. I have, I hope, sufficiently made it appear in my former Letter, that the *first Degree* of this *Disease* was anciently known among us by the name of *Brening*, or *Burning*; and that it was the same Thing with what we now call a *Clap*, The Symptoms, which are usually its Concomitants, are the *Phymosis*, and *Parahphymosis*, both which are accurately described, and proper Remedies, for them set down by *John Arden*, Esq; in another Manuscript of his, curiously written upon Vellum, and beautifully illuminated. The imprudent Method of Cure of this *first Degree* of the *Venereal Malady*, is sometimes attended with a Caruncle in the *Urethra*, which was a Disease very common among us anciently: For not to mention other *early* writers, *Arden* gives us the Case of a certain Rector, who had such a *Substance*, like a Wart, growing in the *Penis*, which he says *frequently happens*, and of another which had such an *Excrescence* as big as a *small Strawberry*, which (says he) *proceeded from the corrupted Matter remaining in the* Urethra. And indeed there is not any Symptom of the *Venereal Disease*, that I find so often mentioned as this of the *Caruncle*, insomuch that it seems to have been more common in those *early Times*, than at *this Day*. But this must be certainly owing to the smooth and oily Remedies they were continually injecting, which, by their relaxing and softning the Fibres of the Part, must necessarily dispose the Contexture of small Blood Vessels, lodged at the bottom of the little Ulcerations, to fill with nutritious Juices, and to extend themselves so, as to form such fungous Excrescences; and so solicitous were they for removing these Inconveniences, that they made use of several Ways by Corrosives and other Methods, to accomplish this end; and a very early Writer among us, has given a very methodical and curious Tract on this Subject, wherein he recommends the removing them by the *medicated-Candle*, which we use at this Day, and lays down divers other Instructions, in relation to it, which makes it probably the best Discourse on this Subject, that was ever yet written. He takes notice of those *contumacious-Ulcers*, which happen upon the *Glans* and the neighbouring Parts, which we now call *Shankers*; and the great Trouble our ancient Authors found in attempting their Cure, sufficiently discover them to have had their Original from a Venereal Infection. These several Symptoms of the *Venereal-Malady* our *early* Writers are very full in their Accounts of, and others, when the *Disease* was in a more confirmed State, to which they appropriated particular Names, perhaps more significant and expressive than those imposed by *modern* Authors. Thus the *Buboes* in the *Groin* they called *Dorsers*, which I have given a Reason for before; and the *Venereal-Nodes* on the *Shin-Bones* they termed the *Boon-haw*, which gives us a perfect Idea, not only of the Part affected, but after what manner it was diseased; for the old English Word *Hawe*, signified a Swelling of any Part. Thus for instance, a little Swelling upon the *Cornea*, was anciently called the *Hawe* in the *Eye*; and the Swelling that frequently happens on the Finger, on one side the Nail, was called the *White-Hawe*, and afterwards *Whitflaw*. The *Process* this Author recommends, for the Cure of the *Boon* or *Bone-Hawe*, is by making use of a Plaister, which had a Hole cut in the midst, to circumscribe it; and applying a *Caustic* of unslacked Lime, and black Soap incorporated together; which Plaister and Bandage were to be secured on the part 4 Hours, and longer, if that was not found sufficient: After this he proceeds to the separating the *Slough, &c.* This Practice of his seems to have been found out by accident. For he tells us, when he was a young Practitioner, he having applyed both the Natural and Artificial *Arsenic* to the Leg of a Man, who was his Patient, it so mortified the Flesh, as surprized him; but by proper Digestives, the *Eschar* coming off, and leaving the Bone bare, he scraped it with an Instrument for several Days, and drest it with Incarnatives, designing to have ingendred Flesh on it; but this proving unsuccessful, he continued to scrape it, till he observed it move under the Instrument; after which having separated it, he found the Sore covered with new Flesh, and that the Bone was 4 Inches in length, 2 in breadth, and very thick, upon the Removal of which the Patient was soon cured. Thus it's probable this Observation of this great Man led our Predecessors to practice the very same Method; and we do at *this Day* in our Hospitals treat the *Venereal Nodes* on the *Shins* exactly as is here described, where we observe the same Appearances, he so long before took notice of; and it is not in the least to be doubted, but the *Boon-Haw* and our *Venereal Nodes* are the same *Disease*. By the Appearance of some of the last of these Symptoms, we infallibly judge the Patient has had the Infection upon him a considerable time, and that the *Disease* is making its gradual Advances, to the corrupting and destroying the whole Frame of the Body. That this was the Conclusion of the Miseries of those Persons, who gave themselves up to the deceitful-Delights and Entertainments of lewd-Women, in those *early-times* as well as *now*, I cannot better prove than by those remarkable Instances you quoted from a MS. in *Lincoln*-Colledge, in *Oxon*, Viz. *Novi enim ego Magister* Thomas Gascoigne, *licet indignus sacræ Theologiæ Doctor, qui hæc scripsi & collegi, diversos viros, qui mortui fuerunt ex putrefactione membrorum suorum genitalium & corporis sui; quæ corruptio & putrefactio, ut ipsi dixerunt, causata fuit per exercitium copulæ carnalis cum mulieribus. Magnus enim dux in Anglia, scil.* J. de Gaunt, *mortuus est ex tali putrefactione membrorum genitalium, & corporis sui, causatâ per frequentationem mulierum. Magnus enim fornicator fuit, ut in toto Regno Angliæ divulgabatur, & ante mortem suam jacens sic infirmus in lecto, eandem putrefactionem Regi; Angliæ Ricardo secundo ostendit, cum idem Rex eundem Ducem in suâ infirmitate visitavit; & dixit mihi qui ista novit unus fidelis sacræ Theologiæ Baccalaureus. Willus etiam longe vir maturæ ætatis & de civitat. Londonii, mortuus est ex tali putrefactione membrorum suorum genitalium, & corporis sui, causatâ per copulam carnalem cum Mulieribus, ut ipsemet pluries confessus est ante mortem suam, quum manu sua propria eleemosynas distribuit, ut ego novi, anno Dni. 1430.* Now what those Instances mentioned from *Arden*, or these from *Gascoigne*, who was then Chancellor of *Oxford*, could possibly be, but *Venereal-Cases*, I would be obliged to any body to inform me. Certain it is, no *Disease* was ever known to be gotten by the carnal Conversation of Women, which first attacked the *Genitals*, causing a Corruption and Putrefaction of them, and afterward of the whole Frame of the Body, but that which is

Venereal. For nothing is more commonly known at this Day, than that after the Venereal-Engagement with an impure Woman, the *Penis* is the Part where the Scene is first laid for the succeeding Tragical Appearances; and there, and in the Neighbouring Parts, do the Symptoms of the Disease, as its Retainers, always first assemble, till the malignant Poison taint the Blood and other Juices; which being convey'd over the whole Frame of the human Fabric, if not check'd, soon brings about its total Corruption.

We do not indeed find the *Disease* mentioned by *Gascoigne,* was distinguish'd by any particular Name: But great Numbers must unavoidably die of the *Venereal-Malady* at that time, from the imperfect Knowledge of those who had the Treatment of the first Degrees of it. It must necessarily follow, therefore, that when the whole Frame of the Body had receiv'd a Taint from the *Venereal-Poison,* so as to occasion its breaking-out in Scabs and Ulcers, almost all over its Surface, it must generally be called by the Name of some particular Disease, whose Appearances had somewhat of an Affinity to it. Now if we examine the Nature of all the Diseases, that attack the Human Body, we shall not find the *Venereal-Malady,* when it arrives at this State, to bear a greater Similitude to any than the Leprosy, as it is described by the Ancients: Nay, so great was the Analogy betwixt these Diseases supposed to be, that *Sebastianus Aquilanus* has endeavoured to prove from *Galen, Avicen, Pliny,* &c. that the *Pox* is only one Species of the *Leprosy*; and *Jacobus Cataneus,* a Writer almost as early as the Rise of the Name of the *Pox,* tells us, 'tis not only possible there may be a Transition from one of these Diseases into the other; but that he saw *two* Persons in whom the *Pox* was changed into the *Leprosy*: That is, from having great *Pocks* or *Pustules* on the Surface of their Bodies, from whence the *Pox* is denominated, to have become Ulcerous or Scabby. This particular State of the Disease anciently put the Surgeons to a great deal of Trouble: For they finding that these Ulcers were of a very contumacious and rebellious Nature, were obliged to make use of great Numbers of Remedies, in order to conquer the evil Disposition of them. But they observed that all of them were useless, unless Mercury was joined with them. Now the dressing each particular Ulcer being so very tedious, they ordered the Patients to daub the Ointments over the Parts which were ulcerated; which done, they were wrapt in Linnen Cloths till the next dressing: But after a few Days they were extreamly surprised, to find their Mouths began to be sore, and that they spit very profusely; but they tell us to their Astonishment, that in a little time the Sores became healed, and the Patients cured. And by this Accident it was the Method of *Salivating* by *Unction* was first discover'd, which is in so much use among us at this Day. From these and some other Instances I have given of the Industry and Application of our Predecessors, and with what Sagacity they applied every accidental Hint, to the relieving their distressed Fellow-Creatures from the Misfortunes they laboured under; we ought to be led to the highest Esteem and Veneration of them; and so much the more most certainly forasmuch as they were principally our own Country-Men, who, I can prove, not only from several Persons coming from *Foreign-Parts* to be cured of their Diseases *here*, but for other Reasons, that they excelled most of their Cotemporaries in the Divine Art of Healing. Now altho' those *Foreign-Authorities*, I before mentioned, might be looked upon as sufficient to convince any one, how our Ancestors blended these *two* Diseases together; yet I shall prove from our own Writers, long before those, that altho' the *Pox* was not only among us, but in distant Nations, anciently confounded with the *Leprosy*; yet, so exact were our Writers in their Observations of the Infectious Nature of one Species of that Disease, and describing the Symptoms, as was sufficient to lead any Person to the distinguishing between them, so as to separate *one* Disease from the *other*. I shall therefore *first* enquire into the manner how the *Leprosy* was sometimes said to be gotten in those early Times, and then examine the Symptoms of the Disease, that attacked the Patient. *John Gadisden*, a very learned and famous *English* Physician, who flourished about 1340, in an excellent Work of his, he entitles *Rosa Anglica*, speaking *de Infectione ex Coitu Leprosi, vel Leprosæ*, says as follows, *Primo notandum quod ille qui timet de excoriatione & arsura Virgæ post coitum statim lavet Virgam cum aqua mixta aceto, vel cum urina propria, & nihil mali habebit*; and in another Place speaking *de Ulcere Virgæ*, he says, *Sed si quis vult membrum ab omni corruptione servare, cum a Muliere recedit, quam forte habet suspectam de immunditie, lavet illud cum aqua frigida mixta cum aceto, vel urina propria, intra vel extra preputium.* He likewise speaking still of the *Leprosy*, recommends a Decoction of Plantain and Roses in Wine, to be made use of by the Woman immediately after the *Venereal-Encounter*; upon which he tells us she will be secure. From hence it is evident some of their *Leprous Women* (as they call'd them) were capable of communicating an infectious Malady to those that had carnal Conversation with them; which proves, the *Pudenda* of the Women must be diseased, for as much as we are absolutely assured

Infections of that Nature only happen when a sound Part comes to an immediate Contact with a diseased one; for the Symptoms always first display themselves in those Parts, thro' which the Virulency is first conveyed. Now in a true *Leprosy* we never meet with the mention of any Disorder in those Parts, which, if there be not, must absolutely secure the Person from having that Disease communicated to him by Coition with *Leprous-Women*; but it proves there was a Disease among them, which was not the *Leprosy* altho' it went by that Name; and that this could be no other than *Venereal*, because it was infectious; for there is no other Disease that is capable of being communicated this way but the *Venereal-Disease*, seeing the *Pudenda* are only in that Distemper so diseased as to become capable of communicating their Contagion. I find the learned *Gilbertus Anglicus*, who flourished about 1360, reasoning concerning the manner how it is possible a Man should be infected by a *Leprous-Woman*; where if we allow him to call the *Malignant Matter*, which is lodged in the *Vagina* [*the Womans seed*] we shall find he acurately describes the very first *Venereal-Infection*, by part of the virulent Matters being received into the *Urethra*; from whence by the Communication of the *Veins* and *Arteries*, it is conveyed into the whole Body, after which (*says he*) ensues its total Corruption. Let us now examine the Symptoms of one sort of their Leprosy, for it must be necessarily divided into different Species, when another Distemper was blended with it, in which we observe such a *diversity* of *appearances*; and this I shall the rather do in this Place, because it will furnish us with the next Succession of Symptoms after those already mentioned, as the *Venereal-Ozænas*, the Ulcers of the Throat, the Hoarsness, the proof of its being communicable from the Nurse to the Child, by *Hereditary-succession, &c.* All which we find to be true in the *Venereal-Disease* at this Day. Our Country-Man *Bartholomew Glanvile*, who flourished about 1360, in his Book *de Proprietatibus Rerum*, translated by *John Trevisa* Vicar of *Barkley* in 1398, tells *us, some* Leprous-Persons *have redde Pymples and Whelkes in the Face, out of whom oftene runne Blood and Matter: In such the Noses swellen and ben grete, the virtue of smellynge falyth, and the Brethe stynkyth ryght fowle.* In another place he speaks of *unclene spotyd glemy and quyttery, the Nose-thrilles ben stopyl, the wason of the Voys is rough, and the Voys is horse and the Heere falls.* Among the Causes of this sort of *Leprosy*, he reckons lying in the Sheets after them, easing Nature after them; and others which the first Writers on the *Pox* looked upon to be capable of communicating that Contagion: Also, *says he, it comyth of fleshly lykeng by a Woman, after that a* Leprous-Man *hathe laye by her; also it comyth of Fader and Moder; ann so thys Contagyon passyth into the Chylde as it ware by Lawe of Herytage. And also when a Chylde is fedde wyth corrupt Mylke of a Leprous Nouryce.* He adds, *by what ever Cause it comes, you are not to hope for Cure if it be confyrmyd; but it may be somewhat hidde and lett that it distroye so soone.* Thus we see how our Author, under the Name of *one* Species of the *Leprosy,* gives a Summary of the Symptoms of the *Pox,* and the several ways whereby it is at this time communicated. Now when these *two* Diseases were anciently blended together, and passed under the Name of the *Leprosy* only, it must be the real Cause why that *Disease* seemed to be so *rife* formerly; for *two* Distempers passing under *one* Name must necessarily make it more taken notice of and much more frequent; not but that much the greater Number of those who were formerly said to be *Leprous* were really *Venereal,* seems to be very evident; for since that *Disease* has been separated from the *Leprosy,* it has drawn off such vast Numbers, that the *Leprosy* is become as it were a perfect Stranger to us. Those who are acquainted with our English History well know the great Provision which was anciently made throughout all *England* for *Leprous-Persons,* insomuch that there was scarce a considerable Town among us but had a *Lazar-House* for such diseased. In a Register which belonged to one of these Houses, I find there were in *Hen.* the VIIIth's time 6 of them near *London,* (*viz,*) at *Knight's-Bridge, Hammersmith, Highgate, Kingsland,* the *Lock,* and at *Mile-end,* but about 40 Years before I find but 4 mentioned: and in 1452 in the Will of *Ralph Holland,* Merchant-Taylor, registred in the Prerogative Office, mention is made but of 3, which, with his Legacies to them, are as follow. *Item lego Leprosis de Lokes, extra Barram Sti Georgii 20s. Item lego Leprosis de Hackenay* (which is that at *Kingsland) 20s. Item lego Leprosis Sti Egidii extra Barram de Holborn 40s,* from which it is worth while to note, that the *Lock* beyond St. *Georges* Church, and that at *Kingsland,* are at this time applyed to no other use than for the Entertainment and Cure of such as have the *Venereal-Malady.* Some of our learned Antiquaries have been much concerned to know the Cause why the *Leprosy* shou'd be so common in those early times, and so little known among us now: But I believe the Reason will be impossible to be assigned, unless we allow, according to the Proofs which I have already brought, that the *Venereal-Disease* was so blended with it, as to make up the Number of the diseased. It seems to have been the same thing with them in *France* as with us: For *Mezeray* tells us, that the House of the *Fathers* of the *Mission* of St.

Lazarus, was formerly an *Hospital* for *Leprous-People*, but that Disease being ceased in this last Age (since the *Pox* has been separated from it) these *Lazar-Houses* have been converted to other Uses; and it may not be perhaps foreign to my purpose to take notice that the Writ *de Leproso amovendo* contained in the *Register of Writs* was (according to *Coke* upon *Littleton*) to prevent Leprous Persons associating themselves with their Neighbours, who appear to be so by their Voice and their Sores; and the Putrefaction of their Flesh; and by the Smell of them. Well then, let us examine what Method was to be taken to prevent this noysom and filthy Distemper, the Leprosy; why truly that which would infallibly prevent their getting the *Pox* after the usual Method, and that was Castration. It is certain that *Eunuchs* are rarely or never troubled with the Leprosy, according to *Monsieur le Prestre*, a Councellor in the Parliament of *Paris*, who has these Words, *Antipathia vero Elephantiasis veneno resistit: Hinc Eunuchi & quicunque sunt mollis, frigidæ & effeminatæ naturæ nunquam aut raro Lepra corripiuntur, & quidem quibus imminet Lepræ periculum de consilio medicorum sibi virilia amputare permittitur.* (Cent. I. Cap. 6. de Separatione ex causa Luis Venerea.) And *Mezeray* says, he has read in the Life of *Philip* the *August*, that some Men had such Apprehensions of the *Leprosy*, (that shameful and nasty Distemper) that to preserve themselves from it, they made themselves *Eunuchs*. Now it is highly probable that those Persons who submitted to such a painful Operation, having before observed, that those who gave themselves up to a free and unrestrained use of Women, fell at length under such unhappy circumstances; and so found the only measures to preserve themselves from it was to be disabled for such engagements, which sufficiently proves this Species of the *Leprosy* was infectious; and for the reasons before assigned could be no other than *Venereal*; for how the true *Leprosy* should be prevented by such means will be, I believe, impossible for any Person to determine. There yet remains one very considerable Symptom of the *Venereal-Malady* for me to take notice of, because it is looked upon to be the most remarkable in that Disease, which, is the falling of the Nose; but since it has been already proved, that this Disease when it had arrived to such a pitch as to discover it self by those direful Symptoms, as are the immediate forerunners of this, was by the Ancients confounded with the *Leprosy*, and called by that Name, it must be among the Symptoms of that *Disease* we are the most likely to meet with it, if any such thing as the falling of the Nose was known among them. Now the most likely Method of coming to a certain Knowledge of the Infallible

Symptoms of the *Leprosy* of the Ancients in its more confirmed State, is to consult the Examinations those unhappy Persons were obliged to undergo, before they were debarred the Conversation of Human Society, and committed to close confinement: But this being a thing some Ages since laid aside, no Author that I know of having the particular History of it, I shall do it as briefly as I can from what Remains I have met with in Records, and other scattered Papers. First then, after the Persons appointed to examine the Diseased had comforted them, by telling them this Distemper might prove a Spiritual Advantage; and if they were found to be *Leprous*, it was to be looked upon as their Purgatory in this World; and altho' they were denied the World, they were chosen of God: the Person was then to swear to answer truly to all such Questions as they should be asked; but the Examiners were very cautious in their Inquiries, lest a Person who was not really *Leprous* should be committed, which they looked upon to be an almost unpardonable Crime: They considered the Signs as *Univocal*, which properly belonged to that Disease, or *Equivocal*, which might belong to another, and did not, upon the appearance of *one* or *two* Signs, determine the Person to be a *Lazar*; and this I find to be the Case of the Wife of *John Nightingale* Esq; of *Brentwood* in *Essex*, who in the Reign of *Edw.* the IVth, *An.* 1468, being reported to be a *Lazare*, and that she did converse and communicate with Persons in public and private Places, and not (according to custom) retire herself, but refused so to do, was accordingly examined by *William Hattecliff, Roger Marcall*, and *Dominicus de Serego* the Kings Physicians; but they upon strict Inquiry adjudged her not to be *Leprous*, by reason the Appearances of the Disease were not sufficient: Some of the Questions put to the *Leprous-Persons*, which will more fully confirm what I have before advanced, I shall now give as I transcribed them from an Ancient Book of Surgery, *yf there were any of his lygnage that he knew to be* Lazares *and especially their Faders and Moders; for by any other of their Kynred they ought not to be* Lazares, *then ought ye to enquire yf he hath had the Company of any lepress Woman, and yf any* Lazare *had medled with her afore him; and lately because of the infect matter and contagyous filth, that she had received of him. Also his nostrils be wyde outward, narrow within and gnawn. Also yf his lips and gummes are foul stynking and coroded, Also yf his voice be horse, and as he speaketh in the nose.* Now the Signs which are here mentioned, were looked upon to be *Univocal*: And these were they who made the *Examiners* principally determine the Persons to be *Leprous*; but what Determinations any one would immediately give from such Symptoms now, no Person is surely ignorant of. But even these certain appearances would not always satisfy some Persons, if we may believe *Fælix Platenus* in his *Medicinal* and *Chirurgical Observations, Lib.* 3. who tells us, some did not look upon them to be so, till they had an horrible aspect, were *hoarse* and *Noses* fell. Likewise in the *Examen Leprosorum* printed in the *De Chirurgia Scriptores Optimi*, the Author speaking of the *Signs* of the *Leprosy* relating to the *Nose*, begins thus, *Si nares exterius secundum exteriorem partem ingrossentur, & interius constringantur, & coarctentur, secundo si appareat cartilaginis in medio corosio, et casus ejus significat Lepram incurabilem.* And the before mentioned *John Gadisden* in his Chapter *de Lepra* says as follows, *Signa confirmationis etiam incurabiliter sunt corrosio cartilaginis quæ est inter foramina & casus ejusdem.* Thus, Sir, have I proved we had a Distemper amongus some hundreds of Years before the *Venereal-Disease* is said to have been known in *Europe*, which was called the *Burning*; that this *Burning* was *Infectious*, and that it was the *first Degree* of the *Venereal Disease*; that this being common at that time, from their Method of Treatment; the *Pox* must be unavoidable: That it had exactly the same Appearances it has now, altho' they were generally called by *different* Names, that the Ancients confounded it with the *Leprosy*; that the vast Numbers of *Leprous-Persons* among us, before the *Venereal-Disease* was separated from it, and the small Number we observe at this Time, is a flagrant Proof of the former; that in describing the *Symptoms* of the *Leprosy*, they give us those of the *Venereal Malady*; and, by mentioning how it is communicated, they describe the Ways by which the *Pox* is gotten at this Day; that such Remedies were by them recommended to prevent the *first* Attack of the *Leprosy*, as are at this Time in Use to prevent the *first* Symptoms of the *Pox*; and that the falling of the *Nose*, which has been look'd upon to be the most remarkable Symptom of the *Venereal-Disease*, was commonly observed in what they called the *Leprosy* in former Ages.

> *I am, Sir,*
> *Yours, &c.,*
> WILLIAM
> BECKETT.